beastly tales

Vol.13 of Indian Creek Anthology Series

© 2006 Southern Indiana Writers

Beastly Tales
Volume 13 of the Indian Creek Anthology Series

Published by Southern Indiana Writers, 2200 Reno Ave., New Albany, IN, 47150
Book designed by T. Lee Harris

ISSN 1085-357X
ISBN 978-0-6151-4005-6

Cover Art and design by T. Lee Harris

To Luci
and all the beloved pets.

Contents

Wanting the Fish

by
T. Lee Harris

The fish were laughing at me. They gathered in the shadow of my papyrus boat, waiting for the next entertainment. I situated my feet on the sides of the canoe, and gripped the spear firmly – which must've twitched the attached cord, because it suddenly jerked backwards. Turning, I disengaged the cord from the teeth and claws of the large, playfully growling cat. "Neffi! Get off!" Rippling spotted fur in satisfaction, he sauntered to the back of the boat and flattened himself over the bundled stems where he watched the gathered fish, tail lashing. "Nefer-Djenou-Bastet! You have got to be the most unhelpful animal in the two lands. I'll never catch a fish if you keep doing that."

It took some effort to put the cord right, but at last, I was standing again, spear poised, reviewing the morning's instructions: Hold it firmly, but not too tightly, let the shaft be an extension of your arm, and most of all, *want* that fish!

In the distance, a shout of triumph rang out, a reminder of why I was upstream from the rest of the hunting party where only the fish laughed at me. Rekhi-mi-re, grandson of the divine Ramesses II (Life, Prosperity and Health for a million years), priest of Amun and all around fathead, had obviously speared a prize. I gritted my teeth, concentrated on the biggest, most obnoxious fish below and hove the weapon. It splashed into the water clumsily and the fish scattered.

"Sitehuti, that was the most piss-poor spear throw I've ever witnessed. If you were in the army, you wouldn't be for long."

I looked toward the riverbank where the shout originated. Djedmose, captain of Crown Prince Merenptah's Medjay contingent stood there, arms folded, grinning. I reeled in my empty fishing spear. "Then it's a good thing I'm not a soldier, isn't it? I seem to be constantly reminding people I'm a scribe, not what they think I ought to be."

He laughed. "Well, you win your argument for not being a fisherman."

"If you want a fish written about or drawn and painted, I'm your man. If you want one caught–"My tirade was interrupted by a splash and sudden flopping in the bottom of the boat. Glancing around in surprise I found Neffi licking a wet paw standing over a large fish thrashing against the papyrus.

"–you'll have your magic cat do it." If Djedmose's grin had gotten any wider, the top of his head would have fallen off.

I fumbled the oar-pole; it splashed into the water and drifted out of reach. Angrily, I snatched the spear and used it to pole the boat to shore.

The Nubian hauled me in with insulting ease and took possession of the weapon. "Where's the boy who was supposed to be steering your boat?"

I glared at Neffi, who purred and headbutted my leg. Djedmose followed my gaze and chuckled. "The Sacred One again?" He flung the spear out, deftly snared the errant pole and reeled them both in, his face clouding slightly. "Regardless, that boy'll get a hiding for leaving you. It's not safe to be out here alone. There are hippos just down river and Si-Montu says he heard a crocodile chuffing this morning."

"I so love the outdoors." Raucous shouts and laughter echoed back to us. "Remind me why I'm here again."

Some of the Medjay's good humor returned. He mimicked his deepest court bow. "It is a reward for services rendered to the royal house, O most-favored Sitehuti of Western Thebes — Life, Prosperity and Health to you!" He laughed and straightened. "Most courtiers would kill to be where you are."

Courtier. Every scribe dreamed of being a courtier. I did too, but it had always involved working toward it by transcribing letters and documents of state. Somehow, I'd achieved it before even graduating scribal school simply by being adopted by a cat. Granted, Nefer-Djenou-Bastet was special, even for a temple cat. His markings linked him to the great guardian cat of Re as well as being sacred to Bastet, herself. When he chose me to be his companion, the High Priest of the temple, Pedibastet (who was also the brother-in-law of the crown prince) decided that made me special, too, which changed my life in ways that never entered my dreams.

Captain Djedmose of the Royal Medjay was one of those ways. When we first met, he'd been sent to my Master's house to escort me into the presence of Crown Prince Merenptah. At the time I'd thought he was going to kill me. So did he. Instead, we ended up working together, much to his irritation.

I wasn't real happy about it either, but for different reasons. The Royal house of Userma'atre Setepenre Ramesses Meriamon had problems and it seemed evident to everyone but me, that I'd been tapped by the gods themselves to unravel them. That was Neffi's fault. It's *always* Neffi's fault. At least he'd come through each time and pointed the way to the solution. I'd be dead several times over if he hadn't.

Djedmose had a hand in saving my sorry skin on multiple occasions, too. Oddly enough, that seemed to change his attitude greatly. He originally saw Neffi as a stupid animal his superiors were reading too much into and me as a social-climbing wannabe aristocrat. He now viewed Neffi with a type of respect and me as a sort of troublesome younger brother. That worked for me. I was the youngest of my siblings; I was used to being treated that way. I was trading on that attitude when I turned back to him. "Not to sound ungrateful, but what was wrong with a nice gold necklace?"

"Anyone can have a gold necklace, Scribe. His Highness, Merenptah, and his Eminence, Pedibastet, wanted to give you something special. You know how they both love hunting and fishing. They hoped you would enjoy it, too."

"Guess I'm just not the rugged type." More shouting and hooting echoed from the camp. I grimaced. "Sounds more like a troupe of baboons than the flower of aristocracy."

Djedmose nodded. "They been giving you a hard time, I know. Have to expect that, though. You're the new kid."

"I have to expect it, but I don't have to sit there and take it. All due respect to the king and crown prince, but the more distance I can put between prince Rekhi-mi-re and myself the better. He probably feels the same."

Djedmose laughed sourly. "You're right, there. He seems to view you as a rival. Senseless, really. Even if you wanted a priesthood, it isn't like they're in short supply. It doesn't help that it's his own grandfather through his uncle who is bestowing honors on you." He paused in looping the javelin's return line. "If you want the truth, he's not the one who worries me. It's that friend of his, Setnacht. That boy is just reckless. Been talking about going after the hippos himself ever since he overheard Si-Montu telling me about them."

"That's not reckless, that's insane!"

Djedmose gave me a startled look.

I couldn't suppress a shudder. "Hey, I didn't see much hunting growing up in the desert at the Place of Truth, but I did see a couple of ritual hippopotamus hunts. I was young, but the memory of those huge, angry animals charging barges is very vivid. Terrified me. Gave me nightmares for months."

"Too true, Scribe. I've seen my share of hunts and participated in a few. Hippos do not go down as easily as that fool thinks." He shot me an assessing glance. "The workers' village is pretty far from the river. Where this bunch played with throwing sticks, you probably cut your teeth on craftsman's tools."

It was my turn to laugh. "By the time I was three, I could put a fine enough point on a brush, the senior draftsmen would borrow me for important projects. Then, I came to the capital and began my apprenticeship with Master Khenemetamun-pa-sheri. Hunting and spear fishing were not in the curriculum."

"We'll have to fix that, won't we?" He handed me the spear. "Okay, your stance is pretty good. We need to work on delivery, though."

We practiced spear throws until the sun sank toward the western horizon. Even with the added encouragement of a revolving number of Medjay who joined us throughout the day, I never landed a single fish. Neffi caught three more.

Djedmose shook his head and lifted the string of fish. "We'd better head back to camp. It'll be dark soon and we need to get these guys to the cooks."

The soldiers bantered about my grip and follow-through all the way back until my head was swimming like a fish. When we reached the pavilions, the cook's assistant whisked the string from Djedmose and hurried away. Rekhi-mi-re snagged the boy as he dashed by and examined the catch, then roared over his shoulder: "Ha! It appears the magic cat caught more fish than you, Setnacht!"

The other noblemen laughed and Setnacht fixed me with a dark glare. He was a minor priest at the same temple as Rekhi-mi-re and had viewed my inclusion into the camping trip with overt hostility from the start. "At least I speared my own. Did you ever figure out which end of the spear was for the fish, Sitehuti?"

Another minor priest snorted into his wine cup. "Don't be so hard on the kid, Seti. Maybe they club fish to death in the backwater he comes from."

Still another jibed: "They must talk them to death where you come from, Un'e, but the ones here weren't listening." Laughter erupted and the conversation thankfully veered away from me and my hunting skills – or lack thereof.

During the meal, I realized Djedmose was watching me. He always became quieter and more formal the closer we came to the camp, but in the firelight, he ventured a wink at me. "We'll work on that follow-through again tomorrow."

I sighed and accepted a cup of wine offered by the camp steward. "It isn't so much my follow-through, I think I just don't *want* the fish that much."

Captain Djedmose was overtaken with a coughing fit that necessitated a big gulp of beer.

I excused myself, scooped up a drowsy Neffi and headed for my tent as soon as I could. This was in part because of the unpleasantness of my dinner companions, but mostly because my pavilion and camp furniture were the only part of this outing I liked.

As I stepped inside and let the curtain fall behind me, the baboons at the fire seemed to recede. It was purely in my imagination. The fabric of the tent walls wasn't that heavy, but with it closed, I was in another world.

When the High Priest, Pedibastet, announced my reward to me, he had mistaken my look of panic to mean "oh no, and me with no camping equipment" instead of just plain "oh no". He immediately assured me that one of his old sets had been prepared for my use. He kept stressing that it was an old set, so no need to be extra careful. I doubted he was even remotely aware that his old and used was better than what I lived with every day. I felt like a prince, myself, inside that tent.

The steward had anticipated me. He'd breezed through like an Ifrit, leaving in his wake a lit lamp, a basin of clean water on the small table and a turned down bed. Neffi wriggled out of my grasp to inspect the bed linens and I had a quick wash, then put the bowl on the floor by a folding chair. Kicking off my sandals, I sank back into the chair and plunked my bare feet into the basin. My feet had been in water most of the day, but this water had the benefit of being wonderfully siltless. I was in danger of falling asleep in the chair. I levered myself up, wandered over to the ingeniously designed camp bed, dislodged Neffi and climbed in. The crisp linen bedding felt glorious and the string webbing below gave just enough. I remember wondering as I drifted off if the Sem-Priest would notice if I didn't return the bed.

The next day we went duck hunting. My skill with a throwing stick was, if possible, worse than my skill with a fishing spear. Neffi, however, proved as adept at catching birds as fish. Maybe a little more so. During the day he brought me two geese and four ducks. Unfortunately, he steadfastly refused to retrieve my throw stick, so I had to go find it myself. The things are curved and are supposed to return to the thrower, but mine seemed to have a mind of its own. It went everywhere but back to me. I take that back. There was the one time it returned to whack me between the shoulder blades. To give the Medjay credit, they didn't laugh – much. I did learn a whole new vocabulary of Nubian swearwords when the stick hit them, though.

From time to time, I caught Djedmose grimacing at my throws and sensed the onset of another hunting tutorial. I was right. We tossed sticks at targets until the light got too bad to see where the weapons landed, which, to the credit of my instructor, was closer to the mark by the end of the day. Still, I was bone-tired and longing for my bed when we dragged back into camp. The aroma of roasted goose woke me a little and drew both Djedmose and myself toward the circle around the brazier.

At our approach, Setnacht stood and violently poked the fire with a stick. It was burning quite well, so the action was unnecessary and inexplicable. Inexplicable, that is, until Rekhi-mi-re laughed and turned to me. "Sitehuti, your magic cat is the author of tonight's feast. The two geese he brought down were the best catch of the day."

Un'e snickered. "For those of us who caught anything."

It soon became apparent from the conversation that Setnacht had no luck with his throw stick. These scions of the noble houses weren't any nicer to people they liked than they were to those they didn't. Unfortunately, Setnacht appeared to be the type who could dish it out but not take it and the jibes were putting him in a dangerously bad mood.

I was wondering where the breaking point would be, when the night was cut by the bellow of a hippopotamus. Conversation stopped and one of the Medjay shifted uncomfortably. "That's awfully close, Captain."

Djedmose's eyes glittered in the firelight as he nodded curtly. "Too close. We better move the camp tomorrow."

Setnacht shook his head. "We're hunters. We should go after it."

"NO. No one is to go after that hippo."

Rekhi-mi-re swiveled on his stool and fixed the Nubian with a glare. "That sounded like an order, Captain. Who are you to give us orders?"

Djedmose folded his arms across his chest. "I'm the man your grandfather charged with keeping you safe, Highness."

Setnacht smacked a fist onto his thigh. "It's ridiculous to move the camp. After all, it's just an animal. My father has killed several hippos."

Djedmose spoke slowly and deliberately. "A hippopotamus is not just an animal, Sir. They are fast, tough and dangerous when angered. There's a reason they're the avatar of Set."

The cook and his assistants charged into the tension with the roasted geese and fresh bread. Brave men. I'm not sure I'd have done it. Regardless, everyone fell to the business of eating and no one mentioned the hippopotamus again. I did notice Djedmose having a quiet word with his men, though.

"It will be a contest." Murmurs of interest greeted Rekhi-mi-re's announcement after breakfast. "We're going to fish again and whoever brings in the biggest catch wins a jug of the excellent white wine from my family vineyards."

The other nobles greeted the prize named with a great deal of enthusiasm and they dispersed very quickly to find the best spots. Oddly enough, the Medjay also melted into the reeds, swiftly and silently until only Djedmose, his lieutenant Si-Montu and I were left on the riverbank. Djedmose grinned at me. "You'd better find your spot, too, Scribe."

I snorted, and sat back down for another chunk of date bread.

I spent the morning fishing in the shallows right by the camp. I had no hope of catching anything anyway, so I figured to stay close to home since the others were gone. All in all, it was an enjoyable few hours. I got in some passable spear throwing practice and chatted with the steward and cooks while Neffi pounced on things nearby. He didn't go too far away, but this was mostly because the cooks kept slipping him tidbits as they prepared the midday meal. They were roasting Neffi's ducks and doing something very interesting with honey and spices.

The others must have been drawn by the aromas, too, because they all began trickling into camp just as the scents of lunch were reaching a peak. Behind me, the camp was filling up. The babble of friendly banter washed over me as nobles, soldiers and servants prepared for the meal. No one noticed me. I was slightly hidden by the papyrus stands, so I stayed put, enjoying my false solitude, idly tossing my spear at passing fish.

Suddenly, shouting and the enraged bellows of an animal shattered the river's peace. I froze in place, then one of the Medjay pelted through the papyrus stands past me. He was covered in mud and breathing hard. He ran straight to Djedmose and saluted. "Sir! That idi–"He caught sight of prince Rekhi-mi-re and changed course. "Sir! Priest Setnacht has wounded a hippopotamus and it has charged him. He's injured but he'll live. The Medjay have engaged it, but–"

There was more splashing, a closer shout and another enraged bellow. Heart in my throat, I swiveled to see a bloodied hippo charging along the same path the soldier had run. Several spears hung from its torn hide. It was heading right for me and the crowded camp behind me.

Time slowed as the maddened, bellowing animal bore down on me. Churned-up muddy water smacked against my legs and I knew I was going to die right there. I hardly remember flinging my spear. I mostly remember clenching my eyes shut, waiting for impact.

The impact came from behind, instead. And kept coming. Terrible screams filled my ears. I finally breathed again and opened my eyes to realize I was not dead and the screams and back-slapping were coming from the Medjay and camp staff. A frighteningly short distance away, the hippopotamus lay twitching in the water, my fishing spear lodged through its eye. I gulped and sagged. The Medjay closed around me, thankfully shutting out the grisly sight.

We broke camp that night. A physician was called in for Setnacht, who escaped with nothing more serious than a broken arm. Everyone was buzzing with my feat and Neffi never left my side. I got more congratulations and praise than I'd ever had. Even Rekhi-mi-re came by my tent and gave me two jars of the white wine. Me, I just nodded and kept my mouth shut. It was the best way to keep from tossing again – not that I'd been able to eat anything. I kept seeing the charge and then that twitching animal in the bloody, muddy water.

I was securing the last of my chests and the steward was folding up the wondrous bed when Djedmose came by. He handed me a cup of dark red wine and ordered me to sip it.

I collapsed onto a stool and sipped as ordered, fully expecting it to come back up. It didn't. Instead, a calming warmth spread through me. "Thanks."

"Best thing for the shakes, Scribe. Trust me, we all get them."

"And thanks for not congratulating me, either."

The Nubian laughed. "I'll hold that for later when the shock wears off more, but you did good, anyway."

"I didn't do anything. Everyone is taking that shot as proof of magic or real skill. It wasn't magic or skill. It was luck. Pure. Dumb. Luck."

The Medjay's face hardened. "It wasn't luck, Scribe. I don't want to hear that crap again."

I looked at him, anger flaring. Of all people, I thought Djedmose would understand.

"You *wanted* that hippo." With a knowing grin, the captain slapped me on the back, ordered me to finish the wine and strolled off to shout the journey home to a faster pace.

Rabbits in Heaven

by
Jeannine Baumgartle

I lie down for a nap, for some reason thinking about heaven, wondering what it will be like...and wake to a field full of rabbits. They pose, noses quivering, in all the prettiness of their kind, unconcerned by spirit intruders.

There is plenty for them to eat. They pallumph casually in the sunshine, the watching and listening signaled by their sentries inclined more toward wind in the grass, and flower nods, and sun-paths that streak into the woods, than to caution. Even bird shadow doesn't disturb them. Shadows here are only quiet, restful places to gaze out from.

I make a bunny chart on the yellow note-pad I brought with me, that represents the earth's responsiveness and, apparently, heaven's, too:

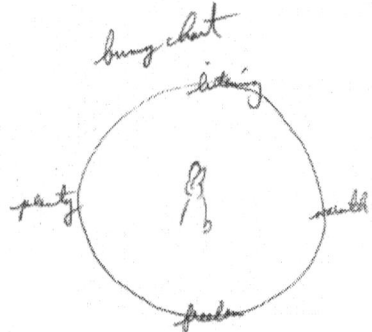

As always, I want to touch, hold the soft furry creatures, but not as much as my spirit wants them to remain wild. A careless imprint might disturb the buttercups as well, and the violets and pussy-willows my longing/memory recognizes from home. –Where wild can live, so can my thoughts. The warm air is fragrant with God's encouragement:

"Here, look at this, lady-spirit, and this," he says, with a sweep of his arm. "You always wanted to know where the magic comes from, how it wakes and blossoms inside as ecstacy . . ."

He smiles that crooked smile of his, and gives me an almost pat on the arm....

Fish and Visitors

by
Marian Allen

Brittany punched John Randolph in the face three times, because she was mad. Then she bit Lavern's foot till her teeth ached, because she was still mad. Then she threw Lavern so hard she bounced off John Randolph and landed on the floor. She was still mad, but she felt much better.

Brittany was four. She hated her name and she loved her Mommy and Daddy. Her best friends at pre-school changed at least once a week, but her best friends at home were always Lavern, the stuffed armadillo, and John Randolph. John Randolph was an inflatable Tyrannosaurus Rex two feet taller than Brittany.

"I don't WANT her here!" Brittany whispered, so Mommy and Daddy wouldn't hear.

"I don't want her here, either," said Lavern.

"Me, too," said John Randolph. "But she's coming, anyway. She's coming today. I heard your Mommy say it this morning when she got you up."

Brittany punched him again. "But I wished really hard on the first star last night."

"That stuff never works," said Lavern. "That's for babies."

Brittany twisted Lavern's head around upside down, but her heart wasn't in it. The worst of the mad was over. When Mommy called her into the living room again, she went, carrying Lavern by her tail.

Mommy patted the couch next to her. Brittany clambered up and sat close, with Lavern on her lap. Mommy opened the photo album across their legs and pointed out the pictures they'd looked at so often before.

"This is Brittany Woods and me when I first met Daddy. Brittany introduced us, remember I told you that? They had been dating off and on, but she just cold-bloodedly made a date one night with two boys at the same time—Daddy and another boy, Bert Byrum—and she talked me into coming, too, and pretended it was supposed to be a double date." Mommy laughed. "The rest is history."

Brittany nodded. "I was named after her," she said in her deep, gravelly voice. All the grownups except Mommy and Daddy coaxed her to talk, and then they always laughed, though she didn't feel like they ever heard anything she said. Inside, she said, *I don't like it that I got my name from somebody else. I don't like it that you got Daddy from somebody else. They both came from her, so I don't like her. If she gave me her name, she might take it back.*

"Brittany, it'll be such fun! She'll be here for a week. It's the first time we've seen her since college, except on the fly at reunions or for lunch here and there. Now she's moving to our town, and she's staying with us until her new house is ready. Won't that be fun?"

Brittany nodded again, but she didn't mean it. She had heard all this before. Mommy and Daddy always told her everything over and over. Sometimes she needed them to, and sometimes she liked it, but she didn't like it this time. She wanted to forget the visit and everything about it.

"It won't be fun," said Lavern. "It'll be awful. I'll hate it."

Mommy went on turning the pages and touching the old pictures as she talked. "She says her friends call her Britta now, so I guess we'll have to get used to calling her that. After all, we can't have two Brittanys in the same house, can we?" Mommy laughed and hugged Brittany. "Her last name isn't even Woods anymore. She married Bert Byrum, so she's Britta Byrum now."

That's better. She has a whole new name. She wouldn't want her old one back, if she has a whole new one, would she?

Mommy turned another page. "I guess she's keeping her married name." Brittany wasn't surprised at Mommy answering a question she hadn't asked. If anybody heard the things other grownups didn't, it was Mommy. "She didn't say, so I guess she is."

"You never can tell," said Lavern, darkly.

The good part was, Daddy shaved when he got home from work and put on some more nice-smelling stuff. It was funny, Daddy having a morning face and morning smell in the afternoon. The bad part was, he was doing it because the other Brittany was coming. "Aunt Britta", Mommy said Brittany should call her.

"Yuck," John Randolph agreed, when Brittany said it with her mouth all smooshed up like she was eating something sour.

"She's here!" Mommy screamed from the living room. "Brittany, come out here, sweetie! Aunt Britta's here!"

Brittany and Lavern came out of the bedroom hall to see Mommy throw open the door and run outside, squealing and talking too loud. Daddy looked in the mirror by the coat rack and smoothed his hair, then he took Brittany's hand and led her onto the flagstones outside the front door. Mommy and a woman were hugging next to a red car, taking turns trying to pick each other up and laughing. The woman didn't look much like the woman in the photograph. Her black hair was short and stuck up in spikes, and her lips were too red. Mommy never wore lipstick that red.

"She looks like she bit herself," Lavern said. "She looks like a biter." That was the insult of insults at preschool. Biters were outlaws, not to be trusted.

"Hi, Britt," Daddy shouted.

The woman let go of Mommy and threw out her arms to Daddy. "Paul! Come here, you gorgeous hunk of one that got away!"

Daddy went and hugged her, but he didn't try to pick her up. He just hugged her.

Mommy came over to Brittany and pulled her across the lawn to Daddy and Aunt Britta.

"And this is your namesake," she said, louder than Brittany liked.

Aunt Britta let go of Daddy and bent over so her face looked too big and close. Her eyes were bright blue and they glistened.

"Little Brittany," she said, like it was the name of a doll she got for Christmas and didn't much want but had to pretend to. "Isn't she cute? Isn't she just adorable? Hello, Precious. Can you say hello to your Aunt Britta?"

Daddy tapped Brittany on the shoulder. "Say 'Hello, Aunt Britta'," he said.

"Say it," Lavern advised. "They'll make a major deal out of it if you don't."

"Hello, Aunt Britta."

"You spiky-headed old lip-biter," said Lavern, but Brittany didn't repeat that part.

Aunt Britta stood up quickly. "Has she got a cold?"

Daddy laughed. "No, that's just her voice. Isn't it a trip?"

"Have her say something else," Aunt Britta said, with that smile grownups got when they thought Brittany's voice was funny.

"She isn't a pet," Mommy said. "She's a person."

"Spikey-head," said Lavern. "Bitey-lip."

"Oh, look at that grumpy little face!" Aunt Britta slapped her own hand. "Aunt Britta's sorry. She didn't mean to be bad. Paul, she looks just like you used to, when I had to back out of a date. She's the image! Just the spit!"

Daddy and Aunt Britta locked arms and went in, chattering in some grownup code. Mommy put her hand on Brittany's head and stroked her hair.

"Let's go give Aunt Britta some lunch, Punkin."

"Yuck," said Lavern.

That was a long rest of the day, with the three big people yakkety-yakking, and Mommy and Daddy just popping into her room to check on her now and then. She could hear them talking about things that happened back in the olden days when they were in school. She guessed from some of the things they said that they were looking at the picture albums, maybe sitting side-by-side on the couch with the book open on their laps. She poked her head out to check. Sure enough, they were, with that other Brittany in the middle, where the real Brittany belonged.

John Randolph didn't like it, when Brittany told him about it. "That's your place. You're the real Brittany. She's just a fake-malake. I bet the red is coming off her lips."

"It is. It's just stuff you rub on your mouth, you know," Brittany told him.

"Oh, I didn't know that."

John Randolph didn't get out much. Sometimes he was allowed to come into the living room for a while, and he got to play in the pool in the summertime, but he was mostly a bedroom dweller.

Mommy gave Brittany supper all to herself, while Daddy showed Aunt Britta his new computer setup. Mommy was cooking something special for the grownups to eat later, with lots of stinky weird smells coming out of the oven and out of the pots on the stove.

"I don't want any of that," Brittany said.

"I'll save a little for you to taste tomorrow," Mommy said. "But you don't have to really eat it."

"Okay, then."

After supper, Aunt Britta gave her a present. It was a book about dinosaurs, with lots of pictures and only a few words on every page. A baby book. The pictures were good, though.

"Manners," Mommy said.

"Thank you, Aunt Britta," said Brittany.

Aunt Britta grinned. "That voice! She just kills me! How about I read your new book to you?"

Later, Brittany showed the book to John Randolph. He liked to look at pictures of himself.

"She can't help it that she didn't know how to say a lot of the names," he said. "Grownups don't know anything about dinosaurs. Dinosaurs hadn't been invented yet, back when they were little."

"I know," said Brittany. "But she laughed when I told her how to say them. She's rude."

"Maybe she doesn't know any better," John Randolph suggested. "Maybe her Mommy didn't teach her any better."

Brittany kept that in mind when Aunt Britta came in with Mommy and Daddy to hear her say her now-I-lay-me-down-to-sleep.

Aunt Britta didn't say anything, but Brittany would have had to be blind not to see her covering her red laughing mouth with the glittery blue eyes all squinched up above it. *Rude!*

After Daddy and Aunt Britta went back to the living room, Mommy bent over Brittany for the good-dream kiss, and Brittany asked, "How many more sleeps before she leaves?"

Mommy held up all the fingers on one hand and two fingers on the other one. "This many."

"Is that a lot?"

Mommy looked toward the door, where loud laughs came from the living room. "Yes, baby. That's a lot."

The next day, Aunt Britta didn't get up until after Brittany left for pre-school, and was gone when Mommy came to pick her up.

"She's checking things out at her new house," Mommy said. "Opening a bank account, stuff like that. She'll be back by the time Daddy gets home."

Lavern didn't come to pre-school, so she didn't say anything. Brittany knew what she would have said, though. She would have said that it was nicer with just Mommy and Daddy and Brittany. She would have explained to Brittany that some grownups made things more fun when they were around, and some grownups made things more like going to get a shot, and Aunt Britta was one of the shot people.

It turned out to be not so bad, though. Mommy said there was going to be a party that night. It was for Aunt Britta, but Brittany knew it was for her, too. Some of the people who were coming were people she really liked, and some of them would bring her little presents because they really liked her, too. There would be more stinky, weird food, but some of it would be good, like the tiny doll's plate of tastes Mommy had saved from last night's fancy dinner. She would get to stay up late, and Mommy would smell extra nice and Daddy would be all morningfied again. Aunt Britta would get mixed up in everything, and it would be like taking medicine in a spoonful of honey.

That's how it worked out. Uncle Pete brought a book about an armadillo having a party. He showed her where he painted out the name of the armadillo all through the book and printed "Lavern" instead. That was the funniest thing ever! Aunt Josie brought her a big piece of chocolate shaped like a Tyrannosaurus Rex. Uncle Arden brought her Trojan War paper dolls and helped her pop out the pieces of a big horse and put them together into a kind of box to store the dolls and clothes. It was almost like having a birthday.

"It's almost like having a class reunion!" said Aunt Britta. "My God, I haven't seen any of you since graduation!"

There was more yakkety-yakking and screamy laughter. There was old-time music, like that funny song about playing with matches that went, "Come on, baby, light my fire". There was goofy dancing, but sometimes Brittany got a kick out of watching big people play. She even started to think Aunt Britta wasn't so bad, after all.

"I think maybe she's a tomboy, like me," she explained to John Randolph. "Every time I see her, she's talking to Daddy or one of the uncles or one of the other guys."

She had to confess her mistake later, though, running back to her room to get Lavern's advice.

"I was in the kitchen, under the table, eating those crumbly things with chocolate in them, and I heard one of the ladies I don't know tell Mommy that Aunt Britta's a man-eater, and always was, and she'd better keep an eye on Daddy!" She was really worried, almost scared. Those red, red lips. She needed Lavern to tell her what to do.

It took Lavern a long time to answer. Finally, she said, "Lions and tigers are man-eaters sometimes, and they have them in the zoo to look at. And sharks are man-eaters, too, but they have them at the aquarium. They're probably safe, as long as you know about them."

Lavern was right, as usual, because Brittany heard Mommy and Daddy talking in the hall later, and Mommy told Daddy, "Just be careful, that's all I ask. Just think about what you're doing."

"Oh, Ellen," Daddy said, instead of calling Mommy "Peaches" like he usually did, "give me some credit for having a little sense, why don't you?"

Brittany explained it to John Randolph. "You just have to be careful. You have to think about what you're doing, and act like you've got a little sense. Then the man-eater won't hurt you."

"How much little sense is enough, though?" asked Lavern. "Does your Daddy have enough?"

"Probably," said Brittany, but she wasn't sure.

The next day was Saturday. Brittany usually liked Saturdays, because Mommy and Daddy were both home and the three of them did stuff together all day long. Today, Aunt Britta would be butting in, though, and that might be dangerous, if they weren't careful and didn't act like they had a little sense.

As always, Brittany and Lavern were up before anybody else. The numbers clock said 8:00, so Brittany pushed the red button on the clicker and then pushed the 1 button twice. "Saduko and Company" came on, a cartoon about a Siamese cat who ran a sushi bar in Chicago and fought organized crime using martial arts. It was too loud, so she pushed the down-triangle until she thought it was quiet enough.

The door to the guest room opened a little way and Aunt Britta filled the crack, frowning and with her face all puffy and her eyes squinched up almost closed and the spikes on the sides of her head squashed down. She was wearing pajamas with Darth Vader on them.

Lavern poked Brittany on the leg. "Act like you've got a little sense. Remember your manners. Say good morning."

"Good morning, Aunt Britta."

It worked. Aunt Britta just growled and went back into the guest room and closed the door.

Mommy and Daddy got up about when Saduko went off, and Mommy watched cartoons with her while Daddy made French toast. Aunt Britta came out in a sweat suit with a wolf on the front and her hair all spiked up again. She went in the kitchen and talked to Daddy while he cooked, but Brittany wasn't worried about him because Mommy kept an eye on the kitchen from her end of the couch.

Aunt Britta went to check on her house again after breakfast, so Mommy and Daddy and Brittany had a nice almost the whole day together.

Then Mommy said the worst words: "We're taking Aunt Britta out to dinner tonight, so Mrs. Ernst will be staying with you."

Mrs. Ernst was great, even though she smelled like medicine, but Brittany didn't like Mommy and Daddy being out away from her with the man-eater.

Mommy must have heard what she was thinking, because she said, "We're going to a grownup movie that you wouldn't like and a fancy restaurant where you have to be quiet."

That sounded safe. You couldn't eat people out in public like that. The police wouldn't let you. "I guess that's all right," she said. "Just be careful. Just act like you've got a little sense, that's all I ask."

Mommy gave her a weird look. "That's a promise," she said.

Mrs. Ernst made chicken and dumplings for supper. Then they walked around the block. Brittany carried Lavern, and Mrs. Ernst carried John Randolph, which was a big treat for him. John Randolph just loved Mrs. Ernst. When they got back, Mrs. Ernst put "Milo and Otis" on the DVD player, and took a nap while Brittany colored in her coloring books. She got out all her old books and went through them, putting red lips on the lions, tigers, wolves, sharks and anything with sharp teeth. She thought for a long time, then put red lips on all the Tyrannosaurus Rex pictures, too.

"I don't wear lipstick!" John Randolph shouted.

"You're a man-eater," Brittany shouted back, in her head. "This is blood. It's cold blood, 'cause you're a reptile."

So that was all right.

She was asleep when the grownups came back and Mrs. Ernst left, but she woke up after the house was dark except for the night-lights.

She lay in bed and listened very hard.

"Don't worry," said John Randolph. "She's up all day, so she sleeps all night. She's whatever you are if you aren't nocturnal. Dayturnal. Besides, I'll protect you."

"What if she's up? What if she's prowling around? Who'll protect Mommy and Daddy?"

Lavern agreed with John Randolph. "She can't prowl around. She's in the guest room, and the door is shut."

"She opened the door this morning."

"But only after she heard the TV. She probably can't come out if nobody else is up."

That made sense, but Brittany thought she'd better check and make sure. Mommy and Daddy liked Aunt Britta, so they might not be as careful as they ought to be.

She clutched Lavern and dragged John Randolph by one skinny arm. He hissed as he slid along the carpet.

Her heart thudded when she saw the guest room door wasn't closed tight. She pushed it wider and crept in, John Randolph hissing behind her. Aunt Britta was in bed in her Darth Vader pajamas, sound asleep with her mouth hanging open.

"Shhh!" Brittany whispered. "We have tracked the man-eater to its lair. It lies helpless before us. If we wake it, we will surely die."

Lavern made one of her eyes hang loose under Brittany's clutch. "Warning!" she said. "Choking hazard. Do not let small children put into mouth."

"I won't put it into my mouth."

"I didn't say anything about your own mouth. It isn't *your* mouth I see hanging open in this room."

"No!" said John Randolph. "That would be sneaky and mean!"

Brittany didn't say anything. She never interfered in their arguments unless they started hitting. They needed to learn to work through their differences for themselves.

"Don't be so prissy," said Lavern. "She's a cold-blooded man-eater. Like a velociraptor. And *they're* extinct."

John Randolph shuddered. "*You* sound cold-blooded, Lavern. Are you sure armadillos are mammals?"

"Pretty sure," said Lavern.

John Randolph shook his whole body *no*. "I don't think Brittany's Mommy and Daddy would like it if we made Aunt Britta go extinct. I think they'd be mad. I think we'd be in big trouble."

"They'd get over it," said Lavern, making her eye looser.

Brittany stepped closer to the bed.

Aunt Britta stirred. "Paul?" she murmured.

"No, I'm not him," said Brittany, in her deep, gravelly voice.

Aunt Britta's eyes flew open. They weren't blue this morning, they were gray, and they didn't glisten. She saw John Randolph staring down at her. She screamed.

Brittany jumped back, and accidentally kicked John Randolph closer to the bed.

Aunt Britta screamed again, slapped the nightstand, and thumped John Randolph in the chest.

Mommy and Daddy ran in. Mommy snatched Brittany and Lavern up and Daddy shouted, "What the hell? What are you doing to the baby?"

Aunt Britta stopped screaming. "The baby?" She opened her fist and a nail file fell out.

Slowly, slowly, John Randolph folded up and sank to the floor.

"John Randolph!" Brittany and Lavern wailed.

Mommy carried them into the living room. "Shush, shush, it'll be all right. John Randolph will be all right. Mommy promises."

In the bedroom, Aunt Britta said, "I couldn't see! I don't sleep in my contacts, and I just saw this big Thing and I heard that deep voice—"

"My God!" Daddy shouted. "What if you'd hit the baby?"

"I *thought* I was being *attacked*!"

Mommy jogged Brittany up and down and muttered, "Wishful thinking."

Daddy came out with John Randolph all limp over one arm.

"I'm okay," John Randolph said, although his voice was muffled. "I'll be perfectly fine, don't worry."

"See if you can get the baby back to sleep," Daddy told Mommy. He patted Brittany's cheek and kissed her head. "You can spend the rest of the night snuggling with us, okay, Punkin? I'm going to operate on John Randolph, then I'll come snuggle, too."

"Okay."

Brittany knew John Randolph would be all right. He had said so, and he should know. What worried her was that Lavern hadn't said anything.

"Lavern is in shock," she said.

"It's no wonder," said Mommy, and carried them to bed.

When Brittany and Lavern woke up the next morning, they were alone in the big bed. The door was open, though, and they could hear the reassuring sounds of clinking dishes and big voices in the kitchen.

"We could go in there," Brittany told Lavern. "We could go around the edge of the room and not go anywhere near that dinosaur killer's room."

Lavern didn't answer.

Brittany slid out of bed and padded down the hall and into the living room. The guest room door was wide open. The bed was made.

"Fish and visitors," Daddy said, in the kitchen, and Mommy laughed.

Then Mommy looked up and saw her and came and scooped her up into a hug.

"Good morning, Punkin. Good morning, Lavern." She kissed each of them, big smacking smooches. "Is Lavern okay?"

"Not yet. Did you clean John Randolph's blood off the guest room rug?"

"Every speck."

Daddy leaned against the kitchen doorway. "Clean as a whistle, and I blew it all back into him." He whistled a few bars of "Dinosaur Parade", the first song on the CD that came with John Randolph.

Mommy gave her an extra squeeze. "Aunt Britta's gone. She decided to spend the rest of the week in a hotel closer to her new house."

Daddy took Brittany and Lavern and gave them a squishy Daddy-hug. "She was really sorry about John Randolph. He's a pretty scary guy, if you don't know him. She thought he was about to extinctify her!"

"Boy," said Lavern, quoting a line Saduko said every week, "have they got the wrong guy!"

"Lavern is talking again," said Brittany.

"Hooray!" said Mommy. "Let's have some Sparkle Flakes to celebrate!"

"I thought we were having fish."

Mommy gave her a weird look. "Fish?"

Daddy laughed. "She heard me say 'fish and visitors'. A guy named Benjamin Franklin said, 'Fish and visitors smell in three days', or words to that effect."

There was more to celebrate than the smelly visitor being gone. There, next to the pantry, stood John Randolph. In the center of his chest was a red bicycle patch, cut into the shape of a heart.

Brittany wiggled out of Daddy's arms and ran over to John Randolph. She hugged him so hard he bent in the middle.

"Take it easy!" Daddy said. "He's been wounded, you know. He'll always be a little delicate from now on."

"Don't worry, John Randolph," said Lavern. "Brittany and I will protect you."

Joy Kirchgessner *Great Horned Owl* acrylic on canvas 18"x24"

Pendy Takes a Rider

by
Bonnie L. Abraham

"Malup's Rebellion occurred during the reign of Deeds," droned Master Colesa.

Gambion covered a yawn with his hand and blinked hard, trying to stay awake. Colesa was not a mage – not even a wizard. He had no magic at all. He had been invited to lecture at the School of Magic only because he was the foremost authority on Malup's Rebellion.

Colesa pushed his wire-rimmed spectacles into place and surveyed the bored, young faces before him. "Who can tell me why the rebellion is significant?"

Gambion shifted in his seat – carefully, so as not to draw attention and be called on to answer. Not that he didn't *know* the answer. Everybody knew the Unsettled Waste was the most significant result of Malup's Rebellion. *Well,* he mused, *a few might make an argument for the splitting of Southern Kingdom from High Kingdom, but not the mages. And, technically, The Waste was the result of Hana Destroyer's ending Malup's Rebellion, but no one blames Hana. It was all Malup's fault.* He shifted again and looked out the window. The sky was that bright, blue-white of a perfect, sunny, winter day and there was one small puff of white cloud to accent it. He sighed. Too loudly.

"Gambion," snapped Master Colesa, "what do you think?"

What do I think about what? he wondered, as he straightened. "I'm sorry, sir. Could you repeat the question?"

"I should think you, of all people, would be interested to learn all you could about Malup's Rebellion."

Gambion felt the tips of his traitorous, pointed ears grow hot. Everyone knew he, just as Malup, had come from High Kingdom. "Yes, sir." There wasn't any other answer to such a remark. He comforted himself that there had been several gasps among the other students at the veiled reference to his High Kingdom heritage. He had a lot of friends in the class, and Master Colesa had just made enemies of them all.

The instructor apparently realized he had made a mistake. "Uh – my apology. That was – uh – my apologies." He paused long enough to remove his wire-rimmed spectacles and wipe them on the over-large sleeves of his obviously borrowed robe. "The question was, what –"

The bell rang.

"Never mind," said Master Colesa to an already half-empty room. "Class dismissed."

Gambion grabbed his book and ran out the door, before Master Colesa could decide to have a private discussion with him.

"Can you believe –" said one voice as he passed.

"The nerve –" said another.

"Gam! Gam! Wait up." That was Felden, his best friend.

Gambion stopped and waited. He would rather not have just then. He didn't want to hear his friend's sympathy, but he didn't want to hurt him, either.

"Sorry about that. We don't all feel that way," promised Felden.

"I know. It just caught me off guard. I'm all right."

"Where you off to?"

"The stables. I still have three more hours of chore time this session."

"I've got four, myself, but I'm assigned to kitchen. See you at evenmeal?"

"I'll be there."

Gambion watched his friend lope off, then continued to the stable.

As he slipped through the narrow opening he had made between the sliding doors, the peaceful silence enveloped him, along with the warmth and smells of the animals. He liked the stable. He grabbed a manure fork and a basket, and entered the first stall – which, to his surprise, was not fastened.

"Good afternoon," he said to the large, brown mule occupying the quarters, to alert him of his presence. "Haven't seen you before. I've come to muck out, if that's all right."

The mule, who had been standing with his back to the door, looking out the small window, turned and snorted softly, stretching his neck until his nose was just in reach of Gambion's hand.

"You're enjoying the blue sky, too, are you?" Gambion slid his hand gently over the soft muzzle, then reached up and scratched between the tall, pointed ears.

Just a little higher.

The boy shook his head, as though ridding his hair of some crawly thing. *Strange. Thought I heard something.*

Stall's not too bad. Rather have a good scratch with a currycomb, if you don't mind.

Gambion jerked his hand back, causing the mule to start.

"Sorry, boy." He reached out again, and patted the animal on the neck. "I'm just feeling a little strange."

S'all right. As long as you go get that currycomb.

"Are you talking to me?"

I don't see anyone else, do you? But I'd just think to me from now on, unless you want people to start avoidin' you. Most of them can't hear me.

Why's that?

Wrong kind of magic.

Oh? What kind of magic is this?

Waste magic. I'm from there.

Waste? Oh. You mean The Unsettled Waste?

Well, I wouldn't call it exactly unsettled. There are people there – and animals, of course.

I didn't know that. So, why can I hear you?

Must have been to the Waste at some time.

Don't think so. Not that I can remember.

You gonna get that currycomb, or not? My back's itchin' somethin' awful.

Over the next few hours, Gambion polished Pendy's coat and cleaned his stall as it had never been cleaned before. Pendy was the name they agreed on when Gambion couldn't pronounce his new friend's real name. Along the way, he learned more about The Unsettled Waste and Malup's Rebellion than even Master Colesa knew.

Wouldn't mention the Rill to him, cautioned Pendy. *They don't like their existence to be known to just anyone.*

I'll remember, said Gambion.

"You've worked well over your assigned hours for this term, young Gam," said the Master of Stables. He had approached so quietly, not even Pendy had heard. "I see The Brown's back."

"The Brown? Oh. You mean Pendy, here. Back from where?"

"You callin' him Pendy, are you?" The old man shrugged. "Nobody knows where he goes. Been gone over a month this time. The High Mage says leave him do as he pleases, so we do. You'd best be gettin' cleaned up. Evenmeal bell just rang."

"It rang? I didn't hear."

Best be on your way. Never miss a feedbag. Master Pols will see I'm fed, inserted the mule.

I'll be back, said Gambion. He gave Pendy a gentle slap on the neck and ran. *Can I tell Felden?* he thought, as he approached the main building and swerved to avoid running into Master Colesa.

Would you trust him with your life?

Colesa?

Your friend, Felden.

Oh. Yes. Yes, I would.

Then you can tell him.

Thank you. Gambion's head filled with a sudden curious longing for hay, and his jaws ached with the desire to crunch down. His mouth watered. He laughed aloud as he realized the mule had just been fed. *Enjoy, my friend,* he sent back.

Rather have oats, came the answer.

Felden was skeptical, even if he didn't completely dismiss his friend's story. Gambion didn't mind. He was still trying to believe it all himself.

". . . so he said I could call him Pendy."

"After Pendrandious? That's quite a bloodline. He was Hana Destroyer's mount, you know. Do you suppose your Pendy could be a descendant of his?"

"Might be. I'll have to remember to ask him in the morning. You'll come too, won't you?"

"Sure. I'd like to meet him."

Before the sky was even light, the two companions stumbled and shivered their way to the stable.

"Do you think he'll talk to me, too?" asked Felden as he pushed open the great door.

"I don't think it's a matter of will he," said Gambion. "He told me most people *can't* hear him."

"Even wizards and mages?"

"He said he uses a different kind of magic. He calls it Waste magic."

About time someone got here. I'm hungry. I'll have a full measure of oats this morning – not just that piddling loaf of hay Master Pols says I should eat, thank you.

"Did you hear him?" asked Gambion.

"Hear what?" said Felden.

"He says he's hungry and wants a full measure of oats."

"The note on his door says he only gets hay."

"Yeh, he said that, too. Should I give him what he wants or follow Master Pols' orders?"

Pendy snorted and turned his back. *Thought you were gonna be a friend.*

"Look at him," said Felden. "He looks like he's pouting!"

"He is."

"Well, I wouldn't want to cross Master Pol – not if you want to keep seeing the mule."

"See, Pendy? If I give you the oats and Master Pol finds out, he can keep me from visiting you again. So I can only give you hay. I'm sorry. But it's probably better for you, anyway. I noticed when I was currying you yesterday that you weren't exactly bony."

Pendy snorted again. He stuck his nose out the little window and pinned back his ears.

"Oh, come on, Pendy. Talk to me."

The mule's sigh only reached as far as Gambion's mind. *Oh, very well. Feed me what you must – today. Tomorrow it won't matter when you feed me oats.*

Gambion sensed this was not something to be shared with Felden and switched back to thought. *Why won't it matter?*

Right after you've fed me my oats, we'll leave. Since you won't be here –

Whoa! We? I can't leave. I have to finish my studies.

They can teach you no more here.

"What's he saying? Ask him about Pendrandious," suggested Felden. "Look, his ears twitched."

"He's just unhappy I won't give him the oats. Pendy, we were wondering if you were a descendant of Pendrandious," said Gambion as he tossed a large section of hay into the manger.

He was my father.

What did you mean – they can't teach me any more? "He says Pendrandious is his father! How old are you, anyway?"

Rude to ask about age, said Pendy as he picked at the prescribed hay. *As to why they can no longer teach you, magic is a great tree. You have reached the point where your branch goes one way and theirs goes another.*

Gambion busied himself brushing Pendy's broad side, and hoped Felden would attribute his silence to the work. *If I go with you, I'll be kicked out of the school.*

What does that matter? Staying here will only delay your growth. You're of the Waste. You'll come with me.

"Gam, hurry up. We'll miss Sams' biscuits," complained Felden. He leaned over the half-door of the stall. "What's taking so long?"

"What? Oh. Sorry. Just thought I'd give him a brush. You go on. And save me a biscuit. I'll be there in a minute."

"I'll save you *one*," said Felden, as he slipped through the doorway. "If you want more, you'd better hurry."

I'm not of the Waste, said Gambion, returning his attention to Pendy. *My parents came from High Kingdom.*

Nevertheless, your magic is Waste. We couldn't speak if it weren't. Try movin' that brush around a little. You're makin' a sore spot.

Sorry. Gambion moved to Pendy's other side. *I wasn't thinking about that.*

I know! The mule snatched another nibble of hay and chewed. *I will have to teach you to think more quietly. You make my head hurt with your yelling. And I don't* know *how you come to have Waste magic, unless you were there at some time. Were you born in High Kingdom?*

No. Here, just after my parents came.

Did they, by chance, come by the South Down road?

Yes, but what does that have to do with it?

Simple enough. Your mother carried you into the Waste on her way here. Now go. Never miss a feed. And come alone tomorrow – early!

"I have to think about that." Gambion returned the brush to the kit and threw another bit of hay into Pendy's stall. "See. You've already finished the first batch, so it can't be so bad."

And dress warm, said the mule. The thought had a definite grumble to it.

Gambion didn't eat the biscuit Felden had saved. He was too busy chewing over the things Pendy had said. The worst part was, he couldn't tell his best friend. If he did, Felden would have to try and stop him – even if it meant reporting the whole thing to one of the teachers.

Of course, the fact that Gambion wasn't eating didn't escape Felden. "What's wrong with you? Are you sick?" he asked, when the biscuit remained untouched on the plate.

The rest of the day, Gambion did his best to avoid Felden. He knew Felden would be hurt, but it couldn't be helped. *I leave in the morning with Pendy, he'll be hurt anyway.* And that's how Gambion knew he was going.

It was still dark when Gambion squeezed through the crack between the big double-doors of the stable the next morning.

In spite of the early hour, Pendy greeted him with impatient enthusiasm. *Oats! Quickly! I wanna be gone before light. Don't like to be seen leavin'.* There was no other communication from the mule until the last oat disappeared. It didn't take long. *Time to go! Get on!*

This proved easier said than done. Finally Gambion turned a large bucket upside-down. By standing on it, he was able to swing his leg up onto Pendy's broad back and then pull himself the rest of the way on using the mule's short mane.

Gonna' have to work on that, grumbled Pendy. *Now, concentrate on the Waste.*

The Waste? I don't know what it's like.

You have the memories from your mother. Concentrate.

Gambion closed his eyes and tried to think what the Waste might look like.

Hang on! said his mount.

The boy felt a slight breeze against his face, as Pendy shifted slightly beneath him.

I don't recognize this place, grumbled the mule. *Try again. Hang on!*

Wait! Gambion opened his eyes. They were standing on a high, flat plain, covered in knee-high grass. The sun had not yet reached the horizon, but its light painted the sky a soft gold. *I can't do it. I don't remember the Waste.*

It's there, in your mind. Pendy rippled the muscles on his neck. *Slow your breathing and close your eyes again. Think your earliest memories of your mother.* He stomped a foot. *And could you hurry? It's cold here.*

Oh, thanks! That helps!

Sorry. Don't worry. Sometimes it takes two or three tries to learn. Just think about your mum.

Gambion sighed. *I'll try.* He closed his eyes and let his mind flood with memories of his mother. Then, with sudden clarity, he saw a vast expanse filled with the oddest-shaped, multi-colored rocks. *I have it!*

No need to shout, said Pendy.

Gambion could feel the mule moving and opened his eyes to tiny slits. The vision remained, superimposed over the passing blur: forest greens, solid stone-gray that was nothing like the warm-colored stone of his memory, sapphire-blue that must have been water. The speed made him dizzy and his stomach threatened to leave him. His heart pounded. Then reality matched memory. Pendy had stopped. The queasiness passed.

"This is amazing," said Gambion as he surveyed the vast, multicolored expanse of rock and sand that had become known as the Unsettled Waste. It was nothing like the flat brown place on the map.

Beautiful, isn't it?

"In a terrifying way, yes." When he had slid to the ground and unbent his legs, he laid his hand on his new friend's neck and stared in silence. *It's so bleak.*

Look deeper.

Gambion breathed in and let it out slowly. He blinked moisture back into his eyes and stared some more. He saw only sand, strewn with hundreds of boulders that seemed to be painted in stripes of muted pinks and oranges and greens and browns. In the distance was a mountain of impossible angles, painted in the same soft colors.

Deeper, said Pendy, *not harder.*

And as he watched the rocks, their marvelous colors shimmering

in the sun as though it were deep summer, they changed shapes. After several minutes, Gambion realized they were also coming nearer. *Uh, Pendy?*

Stay. They are friends.

To Gambion's amazement, the nearest rock stretched itself upward until it was almost man-shaped, and bowed toward them.

Pendy lowered and raised his head in acknowledgment.

Greetings, Pen—- What followed must have been Pendy's real name but it was lost to Gambion's understanding. It seemed to be a combination of gravel being stirred and the bray of a mule. *Welcome home.*

Greetings, Rocgran. It is good to be *home.*

What is this you have brought with you?

He is called Gambion. He is friend.

The rock-man turned to the wizard and bowed again.

Gambion bowed back.

it speak? asked Rocgran.

I do, answered Gambion.

Rocgran winced and placed a small boulder of a hand to his head. *So loud!*

He is untrained, explained Pendy.

Rocgran nodded slowly. *We will teach.* He turned and moved into the landscape, almost disappearing.

Come, said Pendy, as he followed.

Their pace seemed extremely slow, especially after the speed with which Pendy had delivered Gambion to the Waste. And yet, the distant mountain to which they traveled was suddenly right in front of them. Before Gambion knew what had happened, they were surrounded by hundreds of rock-men – and the mountain was gone. He covered his ears to shut out what sounded like a giant landslide, but it was his head, too.

Finally, Pendy noticed his friend's distress. *Peace! He isn't accustomed to this.* And it grew quieter. *Gambion, these are the Rill. The Waste is theirs – or rather, the Waste is them – uh – they are the Waste. Whatever. They cannot be separated.*

I am honored to be allowed to meet you, said the boy as he bowed.

Is he the one? rumbled a pink-and-rose-striped Rill.

It is not time for that to be revealed, said Pendy.

"The one what?" asked Gambion.

There was another rumbling among the Rill, a smaller landslide. Gambion sensed they were speaking among themselves, but he didn't understand.

Will you teach us your ——- The last sounded like a few pebbles rolling down a rock face. The Rill who spoke seemed to have streaks of gold for hair.

Language. The word is language, explained Pendy.

"But, they understand me," said Gambion. He looked at Pendy for more explanation. "How else have we been communicating?"

Mind speech does not have a language. It is just understood. The words you make with your mouth are not the same. The Rill do not understand them, but they want to learn. I cannot teach them, because my mouth does not make the noises yours does. He turned to the Rill who had spoken. *He will be happy to teach you, Goldstone.*

How long will you stay? asked Goldstone, as she brought her hands together with a loud crash.

As long as it takes, said Pendy. *We are not in a slide. Do you agree, my Rider?*

Rider. The word as it came from Pendy's mind expressed much more than the description of someone whom he had happened to carry on his back. It was a title. It meant companion. It meant lifelong commitment.

The little wizard hesitated only a second. *I agree, Pendy.*

The Styrofoam Kitty

by Marian Allen

After sixteen human years of life
Miss Tiffany
—— cat of the silent meow ——
had no heft, no weight, no mass
except on stairs.
There, by force of will,
she mimicked elephants.
Or, when I napped on the couch,
she stepped
down
from her higher perch,
passing a cosmic pressure
through one small foot
into the space between two ribs.

Dixie

by
Carole Wyatt

Gravel thrown by car tires propelled me into motion. "Daddy's home! Daddy's Home!" I screamed, slamming out the back door. Instead of watching my favorite cartoon, *The Flintstones*, I had spent the last forty minutes watching for Daddy. He had left early that day in our old black Buick sedan on the scent of farm labor.

Dad traveled around trying to pick up extra work while he waited for the call to go back to welding. Usually the people he helped paid him in produce, meat, or even livestock feed because we had plenty of animals.

There was a dark shape in the back of the car that I was sure couldn't be a person. Besides wouldn't a person want to sit up front beside Daddy? That was always where I wanted to be. I managed to squirm in between Momma and Daddy on the cracked plastic bench seat whenever we went anywhere.

Daddy stood beside the car with his arms held wide and his straw cowboy hat cocked back on his head. His eyes flicked toward the house briefly and I knew he was looking for Momma. Sometimes Momma wasn't happy when Daddy brought home bushel baskets of green beans or tomatoes.

Then she had to can everything the next day. So it wouldn't go bad. Canning was a hot and messy job that usually involved my older sisters. Daddy had a huge grin on his face so I knew he hadn't brought vegetables home again. Racing across the gravel driveway, I leapt into Daddy's arms so he could swing me around.

"Who's Daddy's girl?" he asked.

"Me!" I said with a yell as if he really didn't know this.

The slam of the screen door stopped the welcome home ritual as we both looked up expectantly. Momma walked out, wiping her hands on her rooster and hens apron. My sisters swirled around her to run to the car. Their squeals alerted me to the fact that I hadn't looked in the car yet.

"It's a dog." One sister yelped. Our two mutts ran around barking as if to add their comments.

"Not another dog." My mother crossed her arms to let us know how she felt about yet another dog.

"Don't worry honey, it's not another dog," Daddy assured her with a twinkle in his eye.

"Then what?" Momma queried as she slowly walked down the split concrete steps afraid of what she might find in the back seat. A weak neigh drifted out of the open car window.

"Not a horse!" Momma's face was red as she aimed an accusing stare.

Daddy opened the car door and lifted out a scrawny, piebald pony that could barely stand on its own. Its head was down as if trying to balance. Ribs stood out from its mud-spattered coat as it wheezed.

"Jimmy," Momma exclaimed in frustration. "You were supposed to get work today, not dog food!"

Daddy gently put his hands over the pony's ears as if it could understand. "I did. I worked at Brown County Auction Yards. This pony was up for auction for either dog food or glue." Daddy knew he had us kids as pony champions as he spun out his tale. "The county brought the pony in because it had been seized for neglect and they were going to auction it off."

"Please don't tell me you wasted our money on this bag of bones!"

"That's the best part. No one bid on her and the state man had no place to take her. I said I would take her home with me. This little beauty was totally free," Daddy declared.

"Whose horse is he?" My sister asked in a wheedling voice. She had wanted a horse for a while.

"First of all, she's a her, not a he. She'll not belong to us we'll belong to her—all of us." Daddy declared throwing one arm wide while he held me up high with the other.

"Hay burner," Momma muttered before she patted the pony.

That's how Dixie appeared in our lives. She grew into a robust, loving horse that often carried all three of us at once. Other lean, pitiful creatures found their way to our farm including the three-legged turtle, all courtesy of Daddy. I learned that day not to judge a horse by its appearance. Through my father's example, I realized that every creature deserves decent treatment and love.

Joy Kirchgessner   *Cougar*   oil on canvas 24"x36"

The Music of Trickling Water
by
Joy Kirchgessner

On a sunny, summer day, in a back yard around a shallow, rippling garden pool designed especially to attract birds, the little feathered wonders gathered to refresh themselves. The human owners of this oasis built a glassed-in patio to watch the activity and surrounded the pool with avian friendly trees envisioning a feng shui- like beauty and tranquility. But realistically, nature has a pecking order.

Earl and Roy, being lowly sparrows, were waiting last in a long line at the pool. Hot, dirty and exhausted, they perched in a weeping mulberry and passed the time chitter-chattering to each other. Earl was a mated bird; Roy was younger and had not yet found a partner.

"I just can't figure it out. I keep in shape, keep myself groomed, and try to bathe regularly," aiming the last statement in ineffectual protest at a female robin who was taking her sweet time in the pool. She was smugly splashing about and savoring her right of domination. She stretched her wing languorously.

Earl heckled her, "Don't you have a nest to sit on somewhere? Those eggs must be getting cold by now." Then he said to Roy, "If we could get the princess out of there, the line might move a little faster."

Roy suggested, "There's a puddle about a mile down the road, but traffic is major today."

A bluebird fought his own reflection in the patio glass. *Thwack, thwack——*
He struck the mirror image rival again and again.

"He's been doing that all summer," said Earl. "He's a few birds short of a flock. Hey Blue, keep it up there, buddy. You can take him, you're *the bird*."

The bluebird took a breather and perched beside the sparrows. "I can't figure this guy out. I've pulled out all the stops, hit him with every thing I've got, seems like he can read my mind. He matches me, move for move. Even sort of looks like me," he squinted at the reflection. "Well, better get back in the ring, see you later." He flew at the glass at full momentum, hit with a splat and slid limply to the ground.

"Oooooo," Earl and Roy winced.

The bluebird quickly sprang back to his feet, "I'm okay. I'm okay." He was back at the glass in seconds.

"We could go up to the big pond, no lines there," offered Roy.

"Not me. I saw a hawk hanging around there yesterday." Earl shuddered.

"By the way, how's the family, Earl?"

"The missus is teaching the kids to fly today. Won't be long, we'll have an empty nest. She'll want to start another brood."

A mockingbird lands in the top of the tree near Earl and Roy.

"Here comes that old mockingbird. He'll poke fun at me." Roy cringed.

"Oh, Roy, he doesn't mean any real harm. He can't help himself, that's just his nature."

The mockingbird moved closer. "How's it going, Earl? You look like you could use a drink and a bath. Found that special someone yet, Roy?" he razzed.

"We'd be doing better if we didn't have to wait to get into the water," said Earl.

"Never had that problem, being of a more impressive size than some birds. I won't mention any names," he teased.

"Here comes the jay," Earl said with distaste.

The jay landed abruptly at the pool trying to intimidate the still-bathing robin. She momentarily stopped and gave him a bring-it-on-if-you-think-you're big- enough stare. He hopped right up to the water's edge, ahead of all the other birds who gave a general moan of discontent.

"Jays. I hate jays. They're always so pushy. Hey buddy—we were next in line!" Earl protested.

"Blow it out yer tail feathers," retorted the jay.

The mockingbird mocked, "Blow it out yer tail feathers."

The jay chirped fiercely, "Zip it, or you'll be sorry."

Mockingbird, "Zip it, or you'll be sorry."

"Why you!" The jay rasped in consternation, and took after the mockingbird who delightedly led it over the house and out of the garden.

Earl flashed a conspiratorial look towards Roy. "I've got an idea. Watch this." He bounced up and down on the branch. "Cat! Cat! Run for your lives!" Earl's chirping was shrill and urgent.

In a pandemonium of fluttering wings, the birds scattered in all directions, some flying into each other, leaving an empty garden pool, sparkling in the sun.

"Heh, heh. I *knew* that would work," Earl said, very pleased with himself. "Care for a dip Roy?"

"By all means. After you, Earl."

Lightning Bugs

By
Jeannine Baumgartle

I love lightning bugs. When the very last shades of sunset become more mist than color, and the long grass is wet with dew, soft light rises in random flares all over the yard. Children are drawn to the momentary radiance, play at capturing it till the moon turns them into sylphs and sprites.

When their parents call them, they carry the wonder inside and discover, as all of us do, that there is more waiting than brilliance. A little bug crawls all over the inside of the jar, wanting a way out, and even the most mercifully grassed and vented container can't persuade him to light up as though he were free.

On the window ledge in the little one's bedroom, the jar remains dark. Somewhere between watchfulness and falling asleep, a slow impulse may come to the sylph, guide it to the window, like a sleep-walker, and suggest a barefoot tiptoe through the night house to let the creature go, back where it came from.

No one else wakes. The screen door is gently opened, and closed by hand. In the shadow of the rose bush, the jar is upended, the crawling bug nudged out. It disappears.

The sylph's return inside is faster, arms clasped because of the chill, a hint of a smile at the small secret to carry with it, under the covers.

Monkey Can't Buy Me Love

by

Ginny Fleming

The summer of my twelfth year, I was truly, madly, deeply in love. The boy was ungrateful and unaware of my preteen passion and yet I worshipped the very concrete he walked on. His name provoked silver bells in my head, Disney bluebirds in the air and happy butterflies in my stomach— put mildly: I believed I'd die without this gorgeous hunk of masculine beauty in my life.

To my young eyes, JT was a dark-haired Adonis. I saw him as a knight in shining armor, a strong, and silent Heathcliff (albeit, a strong, silent and *wealthy* Heathcliff), a blue-eyed Robin Hood to my Maid Marion… you get the picture?

We lived in different worlds. His was Uptown Catholic, while mine was Downtown Baptist. He belonged to the Country Club, while the closest I ever came to anything so exclusive was a membership in a neighborhood gang of knockabout kids; and a scruffy lot *they* were. The wonderful young dreamboat resided in a fine old mini-mansion at one end of my grandmother's street. This poor little rich kid didn't have a mommy and daddy, as I did. Instead, he was raised by *"Mother"* and *"Father"*.

That particular summer, I made every effort to attract JT's attention, but to no avail. In an elaborate grand plan, I wore my slinkiest clothes, which if you consider how slinky a preteen could get in those days, it was a pitiful and sorry sight. In my desperation, I even rode my bike past his house (faithful dog on a leash, loping beside said bike), hoping, hoping, hoping JT would stop me mid-cycle, take my hand in his and ask me the burning-aching question: "Where have you *been* all my life? And by the way, if you're free this afternoon, *Mother* and *Father* would *love* to invite you to tea. Later today, we'll be married in the rose garden. The servants will serve Lobster Newburg and Cherry Fizzies in gleaming Austrian crystal."

Alas, it never quite happened *that* way.

That summer, I tortured my dog past JT's house; around and around, ad infinitum. The dog loved it. Stupid dog. But no matter how many trips around and around the block I drug my poor suffering pet, it seemed the *affaire d'amour* was simply not meant to be. Karma was not my friend, while Destiny was a vicious outlaw galloping full out, trampling my young heart in the city's dust.

Then, as cruel Fate would have it, I was wrenched away from my summer love by a forced vacation in Florida (a visit to my aunt's house in Daytona) with only the sun and the beach to occupy my time. Bummer. Two weeks away from my Prince. What, oh, what to do?

I did what any red-blooded American Angel Baby worth her salt *would* do. I grumbled about everything, made my parents as miserable as possible, and spent money like it was going out of style. I set about on a mission to make the most intelligent choice of how to spend my $10 booty (count 'em— *ten* dollars!!).

I was in a unique situation, being too old for most toys, and not yet into make-up or record albums. I asked myself what would be the most worthwhile manner to spend my fortune, and Myself suggested the Classifieds.

That's where I found him. Joe. Joe, the spider monkey. A pound and a half of brown-eyed mischief and fun, accompanied by two ounces of monkey-doo approximately every half-hour.

Joe and I became fast friends. After our return home, suntanned and spoiled, we took many walks in Falling Run Park next to my home, where Joe would find all kinds of interesting things with which a bright, healthy monkey could occupy his time. That was the Summer of The Humongeous Grasshoppers (it's documented!), and Joe thought every one of them had been placed on this Earth for just one lucky monkey to "bite they little heads off and nibble on they tiny feet". Joe's taste in delicacies sometimes ran to the bizarre and, strangely, people with weak stomachs never seemed to want to eat in his company. Go figure.

The grasshoppers, besides filling an apparent void in Joe's diet, also made a grievous change in his toilet habits. They became very erratic. When you least expected it, "pop" went the monkey— always at the most inopportune times. That summer, I believe Dad considered installing a revolving door on my clothes closet.

If I'd turned up missing, my parents would have given the police this detailed description: "She's short… for a twelve-year-old. Darkly-light brown hair… and myopic greenish-gold eyes. Clothes? Why, yes,

Officer. We're *sure* she was wearing clothes. What color or style? Alas! We haven't a clue! She changes *so* often… Oh, wait a minute! She's the girl with the dirty monkey stains on her shirt!" Dad was not amused by Joe's minor indiscretions.

While moping dejectedly about my Dad's foul mood (constant, since I'd acquired Joe), it occurred to me that Joe might be a useful instrument in my pursuit of JT. So, it came to pass, on a bright sunny morning, at the summer days' wane, Joe and I traveled the ten blocks or so to Grandma's house, a journey gleefully necessitating passing my true love's castle.

My heart pounded as I neared the grand residence. Joe was indifferent, as if he didn't care for this particular walk due to the absence of juicy grasshoppers. Perched upon a towel draped over my shoulder (a grudging concession to my Dad's ire), his little chain in my hand, his tiny hands entwined in my long hair, Joe slumped in resignation. It was a picture straight from the brush of Norman Rockwell: "American

Angel Baby— A Girl and her Monkey".

The sun beat down hot while we lingered… okay— *loitered* on the curb across the street from my beloved's fancy abode. Joe and I bided our time, hoping for a sign of JT's presence. But, all to soon it was apparent, the "Prince" wasn't home.

I sighed and told Joe we'd made the journey needlessly. He turned his tiny adorable face up to mine and made a small "O" with his mouth, telling me with his little "Ooh-Ooh-Oook" sounds he didn't really mind the fruitless walk. It had actually been rather pleasant. Furthermore, he thought I should cheer up. He loved me totally and completely, would, he swore, be mine forever. In fact, I was more than any monkey could hope for… but, could he— perhaps, possibly, if it wasn't any trouble, but only if it wasn't putting me out— have a piece of banana? There didn't seem to be any juicy grasshoppers readily available. And, just what *did* these city monkeys eat, anyhow?

I crossed the street, figuring to stroll past the mansion one last time before checking in at Grandma's house. Suddenly, an expensive car pulled up to the curb. My True Love had arrived in the company of *"Mother"*. The elaborately dressed socialite swept majestically past me on her way to the front steps of her estate. Her perfectly styled hair dared not rustle in the breeze. I could have been a bug on the sidewalk (albeit a bug holding a monkey).

"JT!" she called. "Don't dawdle!"

"Yes, Mother," returned JT. "I'll be there momentarily. I would very much like to see the monkey!"

My heart nearly stopped.

True, JT hadn't mentioned *marriage*… exactly… but, he wanted to *see my monkey!*

Could love be far behind?

"Is that your monkey?" JT asked.

I now consider that to be among the stupidest questions I've *ever* been asked. The correct and only sane answer: "No. I found him wandering the streets and decided: What the hey? Why not give a deserving monkey a home?"

By the time I could persuade my mouth to cooperate with my tongue, which was hiding in terror behind my third rear molar, I intelligently croaked my answer: "Eh… Yeah?"

"What's his name?" my dark-haired Adonis inquired.

"Eh... Joe?"

"Might I hold him?"

Could I deny the love of my life anything within my power to grant?

I handed my monkey over into JT's capable hands. Joe found this new person to be a neat diversion in an otherwise boring day, promptly climbed JT's custom-tailored shirt, and rested on top of his perfectly groomed head. There he sat, forming a tiny "O" with his mouth and making adorable little monkey sounds. JT thought this utterly delightful. One could only imagine what *"Mother"* would have concluded had she glanced out the window and saw her only son, heir to the family name and fortune with a (OH-THE-HORRORS!!) *monkey* on his head.

Now, I have never been *that* terribly religious. But, on that day, the earth beneath my feet quivered and I found myself silently praying as I have *never* prayed before or since. "Lord, if Your eye is on the sparrow, *please* keep an especially close watch on the bowels of this tiny monkey! Forever-and-ever-Jesus'-name-amen!!"

I'm sure I've had many prayers answered in my lifetime. Probably more than my fair share. But, this one has to rank right up there as one of the most appreciated. Joe held tight... so to speak.

Gleefully laughing, JT reached up and gently removed Joe from his head, handing the tiny scamp back to me. "He surely is cute," he said, while I heard the dull clank of broken wedding bells with every princely word. "I shall have to tell *Mother* and *Father* I held a *real live monkey!* I must go into the house now. Good-bye!" I wondered at his manner of speech; enunciating every word carefully, as if I might be *simple.*

The light of my life turned from me, entered his mansion and I was left stranded on the sidewalk, forlornly holding my monkey. I cursed my existence.

There I stood, a heartbeat away from my heart's desire and could merely manage to mumble "Eh... Yeah?" and "Joe?".

I could only imagine JT reporting to his very proper *"Mother"* he'd held a real, live monkey! *Mother— the tiny furry creature belongs to Mrs. Perkins' granddaughter. And, Mother, did you know the girl is sadly feeble-minded? She could only say a few words. Poor girl.*

I sighed a little sigh, scratched Joe behind the ear, gave him a hug and continued our journey down the street to Grandma's house. I was a little lonelier and a lot wiser.

That evening, after much soul-searching, I confided to Grandma (after giving Joe his nightly bath and watching him perform his little, spot-on imitation of Chubby Checker, twisting the night away in his bath towel), I'd finally come to terms with my futile love for JT.

Yes, we did indeed live in different worlds.

JT's was expensive cars and caviar (or so I imagined). Mine was ramshackle Chevys and Lay's® Potato Chips. But, I knew deep in my aching heart, even if I didn't have the love of the "Prince", I did have the complete adoration of one tiny monkey named Joe, and for now… *that* would do just fine.

Someday, I would surely find my "Prince" and when I did, he wouldn't gaze lovingly into the brown eyes of an adorable little creature. This adorable little creature's eyes are myopic greenish-gold… eh… make that *hazel!*

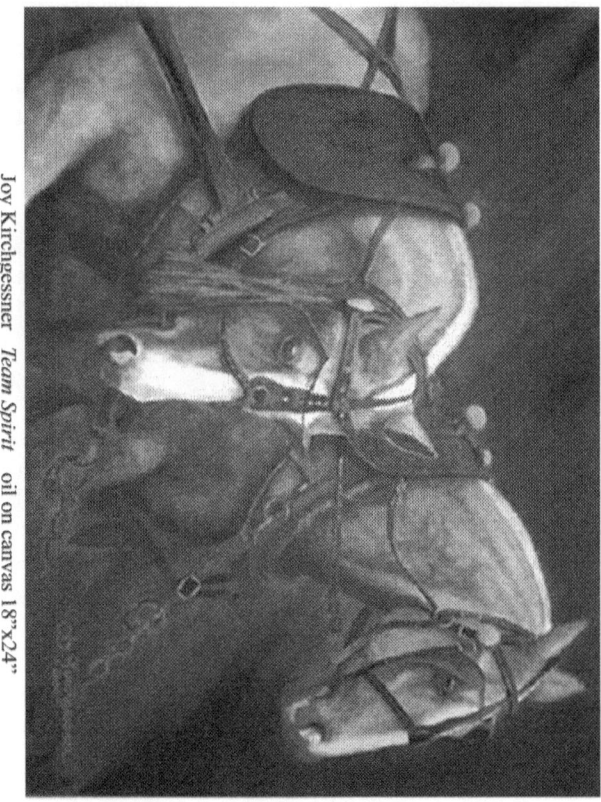

Joy Kirchgessner *Team Spirit* oil on canvas 18"x24"

Totems

by
Dirk Griffin

Concrete drives the animal
Spirits from us
Forcing them to heartless
Limbo
Disconnected
Seeking cool fields of
Grass
Swift winds of
Wild
Wandering runs
Rivers of
Cold enveloping
Waters
Deep forested
Hills

Beasts of our
Hearts were
Never meant for
Domestication
They are the
Us beyond reason

You feel them
Howling
You sit
Silent on their
Desecrated hides
Meeting with
Others denying
Totem voices
Wailing from
Within

Tomb of concrete
High above
Covered
Tortured ground
Coyote cries
Owl calls
Bear stumbles
Drunk with anger
Hawk struggles to
Open pinned
Wings

Stretching sky
Beyond the glass
Sings back
Brother
Sister
Must we be denied
Symbiosis
I see you
Fade
I feel you
Wither
Where you go
I do not wish to
Follow
Where you go
Echoes
Emptiness

The Blessing of Saint Francis
by

Glenda Mills

October 4th was one of Joseph Francis Jerome Shane's favorite days. It was the feast day for St. Francis of Assisi, a man who had found God most profoundly in the splendor, complexity, and beauty of nature. Because of his spirituality, October 4th was also the day for the blessing of animals. Father Joe had spent the cool, crisp morning in the parking lot of St. Clare's, laying hands on cats, dogs, hamsters, fish bowls, lizards, and one very large snake, asking God, through the intercession of St. Francis, to keep them safe and healthy. Now he was on the road, making rounds to the farms to bless the horses, cows, goats, pigs, and sheep.

By the time he pulled into the Worton place, he'd had enough glasses of sweet tea and lemonade to float the Ark. He'd eaten pie, cake, cookies, one breakfast, and a couple of lunches. He was glad this was his last stop. Being cordial was upsetting his stomach. His front seat was already crowded with various jellies and jams, jars of vegetables, and a loaf of homemade bread.

Matthew Worton came running down the driveway to meet Father's car. Matt was wearing his favorite Spiderman T-shirt and denim shorts. He had his mother's chestnut hair and his dad's green eyes. He was short for his six years, thin, and tan from playing outdoors all summer.

"Father Joe! Father Joe!" The boy was shouting before the priest was even out of his car.

"Hi, Matt. Is your mom in the house?"

"Yeah, but I need you to come to the barn with me right now. It's real important. My puppy's sick."

Before Father could say anything, Matt turned and ran across the yard. The priest followed as quickly as he could, considering his full stomach and arthritic knees. Once inside the barn, he saw Matt kneeling beside the bed of hay in an empty stall. He went to the place where the boy was and knelt beside him. Even in the dim light, Father Joe could see the puppy's limp, bleeding body.

"You gotta pray for him, Father, so he'll get well."

The puppy was seriously injured, and the priest knew no prayers were going to save him. His heart sank, even as his mind began searching frantically for the words to explain this to Matt.

"He got under one of the horses' hooves and got stepped on. Mom says he's gonna have to be put down when Dad gets home 'cause he's hurt too bad. I don't want Dad to do that, so you gotta pray for him."

"Matt, I know this is going to be hard to understand, but I don't think your puppy is going to get better. He's badly hurt and probably suffering."

"I know he's hurt real bad, but God can do it. I know He can. He's real powerful. You say so all the time." Matt reached down and gently stroked the pup's soft ears.

"God doesn't always answer our prayers like we want. Even if I pray for your puppy, he still might die."

Matt thought for a second. "If I prayed for him, God might say no 'cause I said something mean to my friend at school yesterday, and He's probably mad at me. But you're His best friend, so He'll listen to you."

"God would never punish your puppy because you said something that was unkind." He placed his hand on the child's shoulder. "There's no easy way to explain why, but death is real and prayer isn't a magic spell that makes it go away. I wish I could make your puppy get well, but I can't."

Matt rolled his eyes. "I know *you* can't make him better. But God can and He will if you ask Him. Please."

Father Joe looked at the trusting face staring back at him and knew why Jesus had said that the Kingdom belonged to such as this. The way Matt's faith worked, it was simple. You asked and God answered. There was no doubt in his mind that the puppy would get well. The priest knew differently. There were no simple answers, and the puppy was dying. He placed his hand on the puppy, and prayed for Matt.

He was on his way back to the car after blessing the other animals on the Worton farm when he saw Matt sitting on the front porch, holding his puppy in a blanket and crying. He could leave quietly and not face the questions of a six-year-old child - questions for which he had no answers. That would be the easy thing to do, but it wouldn't be the right thing. He whispered a quick prayer for guidance, sat down beside

the little boy and waited.

"God is mean. He let my puppy die. I don't like Him anymore, and I'm not going back to church. Ever."

"I'm sorry your puppy died. I could try to explain, but it wouldn't help you understand." He sat quietly for a moment, listening as the boy's sobs relented slightly. "You loved your puppy a whole lot, didn't you?"

"Yeah. He was a good puppy. He played in my room and licked my face. He only chewed up a few things, and he hardly ever peed in the house. Even Mom said he was good. Why would God let a good puppy like him die? If I was God, I would only let mean dogs die."

"You know your puppy's going to live in Heaven now. He'll have steak every day and lots of room to play."

"I don't want him to die and play in Heaven. I want him to play with me." Matt sobbed harder.

"I know, but he can't do that anymore."

"I'll wait 'til Dad gets home. He'll make him all better."

"Matt, he can't make the puppy better. Your puppy is dead."

The boy kept his eyes fixed on his deceased friend. "Yes, he can. Dad can fix anything."

"He can't fix this." Father Joe's voice was quiet but firm.

"If he can't, then he'll take my puppy to the doctor. The doctor will make him better."

Father Joe cupped the boy's face in his hands and lifted Matt's gaze to meet his own. "Matt, there's no one who can fix this. Once something dies, *no one* can make it well again. Your puppy's in Heaven, and not you, or me, or your dad, or the doctor can bring him back."

"I'll get a ladder and climb up to Heaven and get my puppy and carry him home."

"They don't make ladders tall enough to reach Heaven. He has to stay."

"But, I don't want him to live in Heaven with God. I want him to live with me." Matt hugged the blanket close and cried.

Father Joe squeezed the boy's shoulder gently. "I'm really sorry about your puppy."

The next morning, Father Joe went outside to get his paper. There, on the rectory steps, was a beagle puppy. The priest picked him up and received a juicy kiss on his cheek for his effort. He looked for a collar or some type of identification, but found nothing that told him who owned the little guy. The puppy buried his face in the priest's chest and whimpered. All he needed was some food, a good scrubbing, and lots of love. Father Joe took him inside, called the vet, opened a can of beef stew, and ran a bath.

Two weeks passed. No one answered the newspaper ad or the flyers he had placed all over town. As cute as the puppy was, Father Joe knew he couldn't keep him. He'd chewed up two pairs of shoes and whined incessantly at night unless he was curled up in the priest's bed. He needed a permanent home. Father Joe made a phone call and headed out the door, puppy in tow.

A half-hour later, Father pulled into the Worton driveway. This time he didn't have jelly or bread on his front seat. Instead, he had a picnic basket. He looked down and saw a small, wet nose poking its way out of the top.

"Oh no you don't. You'll spoil the surprise."

He got out of the car carrying the basket and found Matt in the backyard on his tree swing. He waved at the boy, who jumped off the swing and came over to where the priest was standing.

"I brought you something, Matt. Would you like to see what it is?"

"Sure." The two sat down on the grass with the basket between them.

"Well, go ahead. Open it."

Matt lifted the lid and found big brown eyes looking up at him from the bottom of the basket. He lifted the beagle to his face, and the puppy licked him on the mouth. Matt giggled.

"I think he likes you. He showed up at my house a couple of weeks ago. I've tried to find his owner, but no one knows where he belongs. I can't keep him. I was wondering if maybe you could help me find him a home."

The beagle whimpered and laid his head in Matt's lap. The boy reached down, petted his head and stroked one of his long, soft ears. "Well, I guess I could see if Mom would let him stay here. He is awful cute. Come on, boy, let's go ask."

Matt scooped up the puppy and disappeared through the back door. Father Joe walked to his car. "Thank you, St. Francis," he whispered.

Queen

by
Jane E. Jones

Queen was found at the stockyards, on her way to the dog food factory, in the early 1940's. She was a sixteen-hand, Standardbred mare with a habit of rearing and throwing herself over backwards whenever something didn't suit her.

My dad bought her for $25.00 and brought her home to our farm near Salem. Eventually, he convinced her that the rearing and falling over backwards was a bad idea, mostly by letting her do it repeatedly, and then making her do what she didn't want to anyway.

I was three years old at the time and didn't care if she had bad habits with the adults. She never used them with me. I loved her at first sight. My older sister and I already had a black Welsh pony, named Billy. From the moment I saw her, I abandoned Billy to my sister and claimed Queen as my own.

My "job" was to sit astride the big Belgium work horses and guide them between the rows as my dad plowed the corn and to ride them back and forth as they pulled the hay up into the loft with the big hay forks. That was boring, but it was a way to get to ride the horses. And besides, the gentle giants made good babysitters.

By the time I was four, Queen and I had a system. I would pull on the sides of her bridle and she'd hold her head down. Then I would climb up and sit astride her head and she would raise it so I could slide down her neck onto her back. She wouldn't do that for anyone else. The only thing wrong with our system was that I would be sitting backwards and would have to turn around. This wasn't much of a problem, since I never used a saddle anyway. I rode her every night to bring the cows to the barn for milking and to take them back to the pasture, which was about a half mile away on the other side of the river.

By the time I was five, I had discovered how much fun it was to gallop on the horses. My dad threatened me with all kinds of punishments, but there was no way I was going to plod along at a walk when we could run. So I would race Queen up the big hill to the cow pasture and thought I was Roy Rogers, who was my hero by then.

My dad kept saying, "don't run up that hill, there are rock ledges that Queen could stumble on." But I knew she wouldn't. Until the day she did. We were going up that hill at a full gallop when she hit one of the ledges and fell head over heels into the rocks.

The next thing I knew, Queen was standing over me, nudging me with her nose and trying to make me get up. I sat up, but for some reason, I couldn't see a thing. Finally, I figured out that this was because my head was bleeding and the blood was running down over my eyes. I managed to get up by holding onto Queen's mane and we walked around in the woods until she stopped next to a big stump. Normally, there would be no way she would get anywhere near something like that, but she stood right up against it and waited patiently while I climbed onto the stump and managed to pull myself up onto her back.

At first I thought I had better go on and get the cows. I knew I would be in trouble if I went back without them – it was milking time. But about the time I got to the top of the hill, I decided I was going to be in trouble anyway, because Dad would know I'd been running Queen up the hill as soon as he saw me. So I turned around and went home without the cows. Queen walked along very slowly the whole way back, even though she usually tried to run when we were going toward the barn.

I rode around the corner of the barn just as my mother came out the door. She looked at the blood running down off my chin from the cut on my forehead and caught her breath. Then she said, calm as could be, "What did you do? Did you run up that hill?" I just knew I was going to get a spanking, but all she did was put the horse away, wash my face, and bundle me into the car for a trip to the doctor's office. She never said a word about it until after the doctor had my head all sewed up and we were heading for home. Then she said, "Now do you see why we said not to gallop up that hill?" That was the end of it.

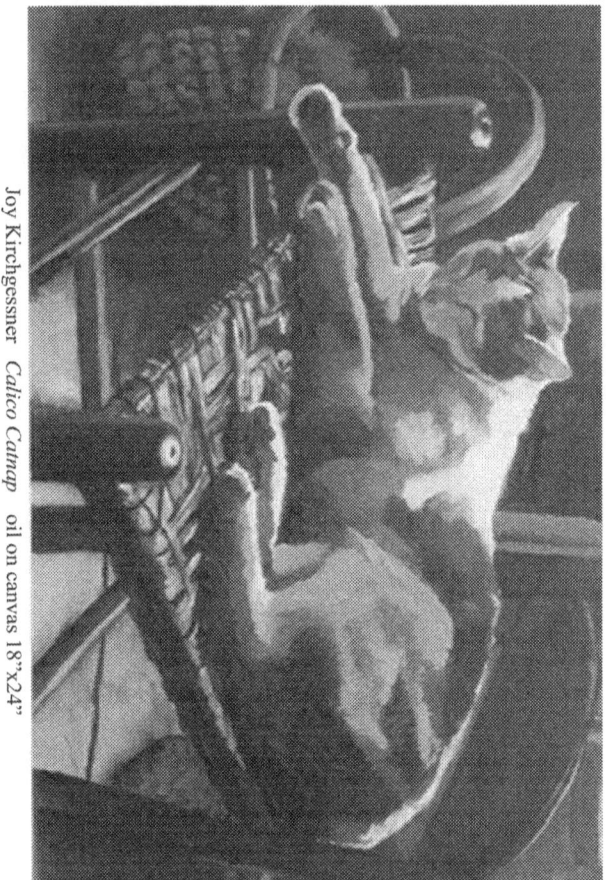

Joy Kirchgessner *Calico Catnap*   oil on canvas 18"x24"

From Outside

by Jeannine Baumgartle

The kitty doesn't understand
about windows. She jumps
when I appear, and slides
down the glass. This
"leap of faith" into my arms
didn't work out, but
she's a brave little kitty
and hurries to the door
to ask why.
I bring her inside,
show her all the presents
under the tree,
none of them as interesting
as my shoestrings.
In the kitchen,
my son drops the plate
of Christmas cookies.
I am tempted to yell,
but Sneezy (the cat)
has retreated in fear
under the couch.
I coax her out,
reassure her with
gentle strokes, and
immediately hold
a purring machine,
better than any present
I will recieve, any
song I will hear.
I hand her to my son.

Transformation

by

Joanna Foreman

According to the rules, you have to live a specific number of animal lives before you can come to Earth a human. An animal can't select his owner; all he can do is state his purpose in life. My purpose was to make a difference in this world. I think that's why Michael chose me. My life as a Siberian husky lasted less than five months, but it was the best time I've had so far. The entrance was a piece of cake, but the exit was the worst imaginable for any animal I've ever known. However, I've only known a few, for I am yet a young soul; if this craziness doesn't stop, I'll never accumulate enough Earth-time to become an old one.

I was eight weeks old and still had that adorable puppy look. In my cage, I waited, watching the door eagerly for someone to walk in and take a glance at me. The pet shop was located in downtown Iowa City, and people came in for all sorts of reasons: bags of kibble, flea collars, doggie treats, etc. A few of them checked me out, but no one really turned *me* on. One day in May, the bell over the door tinkled, and a couple walked in. I had just begun my nap, so I didn't pay much attention. Out of the corner of my eye, I saw them in the bonding room with the pug, so I figured there wasn't much hope for me. If an ugly dog is what they wanted, I had little need for them anyhow.

May 15

Dear Mom, You won't believe what I did last week. I bought a Siberian husky puppy! Megan and I had gone into the pet store just to look around, or at least that's what we thought. I was holding a pug, when I noticed the husky looking at me out of the corner of her eye. I swear, Mom, she sent me a subliminal message to take a look at her, so you know I had to. We spent some time with her, but I was afraid I'd make a rash decision, so we went home. We went back a few hours later because I couldn't get her off my mind! I think I've wanted a dog for a long time but haven't acknowledged it aloud. Puppy kennel, large wire cage, kibble and treats, leash and flea collar, piddle pads and toys ran up the bill. I didn't care—she was the dog for me. When I slipped my credit card out of my wallet, she looked at me as if to say, "Are you sure you can afford me?" I brought her home and she pranced and jumped all over the place, padding through the house, exploring. I showed her where to use her piddle pad, and she knew all about it right away, thankfully.

Love, Michael

P. S. I named her Suzi.

Next thing I knew, the shopkeeper unlatched my cage and handed me to the man in the private room. He was a tall, skinny guy with deep hazel eyes and profuse brown curls that tumbled down his head like a poorly groomed French poodle I once knew. I imagined him to be a student at the university there in town. He told me his name was Michael, but I thought of him as Bob Dylan, because that's who he reminded me of, only much younger of course. (Bob Dylan actually was a French poodle in a previous life). I licked Michael's face all over. He was the one—I just knew it! Then, out of the blue, he handed me back to the shopkeeper and left the pet shop. I was miserable; surely, there was something wrong with me.

Sleep solves all things, so that's what I did. I dreamed of the Antarctic, snow ten feet deep and ice as thick as a house. A pack of eight pulled a dog sled. I was the leader. We bounded forward in sync, and barked, oh did we bark! My paws moved like there would be no tomorrow. Ordinarily, I don't appreciate being awakened from a good dream, but that day I made an exception. The Bob Dylan guy and his lady friend had returned, and the three of us spent an hour in a private booth. I gave it all I had. I wagged my tail, uttered clever little squeals, and offered lots of puppy kisses. When he softly caressed my droopy puppy ears, that's when I knew I had his full attention. I sensed he appreciated a dog with intelligence, so I sat straight up and made direct eye contact. We gazed at one another, and our souls intertwined.

He pulled his wallet out of his back pocket and slipped his credit card onto the cashier's desk. I hoped he had enough to cover it, because dogs like me don't come cheap. I needed lots of stuff, like treats and toys for me to chew on, rather than furniture, shoes, rugs, or anything else, really, that I might take a liking to.

They took me to his house, a big red duplex on Dubuque Street, about a mile away from campus. The ceilings were tall and the floors were hardwood. Michael watched me vigilantly and gave me a treat every time I pee'd on the piddle pad. I drank lots of water so I'd have to go often. More treats for me. I tried to chew on his shoe, then his sofa, and once I headed for his guitar to see what it smelled like. Each time, he'd say NO, then he'd say "toy". Well, so, some things I could chew on and some things I could not. I wanted to please him, so I obeyed. Then, too, there were the treats. I learned Suzi come, sit, lie down, paw and dance. When I felt sleepy, I'd head for my kennel where Michael kept a two-liter bottle of frozen Evian for me to cuddle against. That was my Antarctic and I was happy to be there in my dreams.

May 30
Dear Mom, In your last letter you asked me at least a half-dozen questions, as usual. I will try to answer them here. What does she look like? Well, for starters she is black and white. I'm sending you a picture. Look at those pure white legs and paws and the white lines over her eyes, somewhat like eyebrows. I love her markings, and those sweet floppy ears. And, no, I'm not worried about the landlord and the no-pet policy. The worst they can do is fine me one hundred dollars and ask me to move, or get rid of the dog. In that case, I will move. My lease is nearly up, anyway. Suzi is worth whatever I have to do. She stays inside most of the time since I'm using the piddle pads to house-break her for now. She is so smart, and really hasn't been hard to train, thanks to the puppy treats.
Love, Michael

When I was ten weeks old Michael took me fishing and helped me find a patch of shade to stretch out in. He caught a fish and brought it over to me. I licked it, but didn't care for the scratchy sensation at all. I sneezed and licked my chops to get the strange taste out of my mouth. Michael laughed and threw the fish back into the lake. So that's what fishing is all about, I thought, but I didn't see any point to it at all.

Some days we took walks to his lady friend's house, and so it was that she became my mommy and Michael my daddy, and I was Suzi their daughter. Mommy had saved up her money for a purebred cat, a longhaired Ragdoll; Maja joined the family and Mommy and Daddy sometimes laughed until they cried at our antics. I felt safe and secure, knowing I would live a long and happy life with my human parents who loved and guided me. A dog's life can be a good one if you have the right owner.

It didn't take long for me to realize my purpose of making a difference in this world. Michael was a college student just as I thought, and he was also a creative writer. Like many students (and writers, too), Michael had a problem with late-night beer drinking and poor class attendance. Missed class equals poor grades. He wanted a dog so he could learn self-discipline and accountability. He had tried other ways, such as an alarm clock for one, but to no avail. He knew a dog wouldn't take no for an answer. And I didn't, either. I woke him up early every morning, and he actually seemed glad to have a reason to be efficient. I thought I would spend my entire life as Michael's pet, helping him change for the better. In twenty years, on my next go-around as a human, wouldn't my resumé look good with so much experience?

June 15

Dear Mom, You won't recognize me. Suzi has turned my life around. I have finally found a way to be responsible. In the eight years since Dad died it was a dog that finally got me out of my depressed state. I'm drinking a whole lot less, getting up on time for class, and am positive about the future for a change. I'm writing fiction again, and one of my stories has been accepted for publication. Isn't it amazing that a dog can make me feel this way? I have never loved an animal this much, not even the pets we had when I was a little kid. Can you imagine? Maybe it's because I am solely responsible for Suzi's care. Is this what it's like to have a daughter? I can't wait for you to see your granddog.

Love, Michael

June 25

Dear Mom, I'm glad you came for a weekend visit. I knew Suzi would take an immediate liking to you. It's like she knew you were her grandmother, isn't it? Now that warm weather is upon us, I'm putting a two-liter bottle of frozen Evian inside her kennel when she sleeps to keep her cool. Nothing but the best for my Suzi. When she gets sleepy, she heads for her kennel and hugs that frozen bottle, and I suspect she dreams of the Antarctic. Every day I take her for a walk to Megan's house, and we have taught her to shake hands and dance. She doesn't even need a treat anymore to obey. We will bring her when we come for a visit over the Fourth of July.

  Love, Michael

Over the Fourth of July, we took a trip to Indiana to meet the grandparents, uncles, niece and nephew. Michael showed off all of the tricks he'd taught me, and my grandma and grandpa went ga-ga over me. Grandma took digital pictures while I dogpaddled in the pool and the children giggled. They put on a terrific firework display, and I wasn't even afraid of the noise. On the trip back to Iowa, I sat in Michael's lap and watched the Illinois scenery from the passenger side window. Passersby pointed and waved. I thought people were just the most wonderful of all creation.

July 7

Dear Mom, Fourth of July was fantastic. I was so proud of Suzi, the way she sat right there with the family when we put on our fireworks display in the backyard. She didn't even appear frightened like my brother's dog. I know you must secretly think of Suzi as your favorite granddog, don't you? Thanks for the photographs and puppy toys. The pink pig with the squeak in its tail is her favorite. Here is a picture of her, now that her ears are pointing upward, which somehow happened overnight.

Love, Michael

On July 31 Michael went fishing in the hot, late afternoon, but he left me at home in air-conditioning with my frozen Evian. I dreamed my favorite dreams, until I heard Michael enter the back door. I stood up and barked, calling him to come for me, but it wasn't Michael at all. A stranger with a dark hooded jacket came to my kennel and opened it. I had no idea what he was up to, but from the look on his face I suspected it wasn't good. My intuition saw evil written all over him. I growled and whined a little, and looked up at him with distrust. He grabbed me by the scruff of my neck and lifted me six feet off the floor, then slammed me down hard. I yelped and ran from him, but he chased me, and kicked me halfway across the dining room floor. I lay there, stunned, wondering what to do. He broke each of my four legs, one after another, and kicked me a few more times for good measure. He walked out of our home, leaving me crumpled and discarded on the dining room floor. I couldn't feel anything, nor could I move my legs, but there was no more pain. I was numb. I floated in and out of consciousness until Michael came home. He ran to me and scooped me up into his arms and took me to the vet, where they scanned and x-rayed me, and gave him the really bad news. They placed me underneath an oxygen tent in Intensive Care, where I remained all night long. I tried to hang on, I really did, but I died at nine o'clock the next morning from internal bleeding.

August 1
Dear Mom, The most horrible thing has happened to Suzi. Yesterday

I went fishing and left her in her kennel. When I got back, the kitchen door was unlatched, but I didn't think much about it at first. Then I found Suzi on the dining room floor, unconscious. I thought maybe she had suffered a stroke or something. I took her in my arms, straight to the vet, who gave me the bad news. Someone had entered my home and savagely beat her and left her there, alone and forsaken. How could this be? I can't help but wonder about the landlord and the no-pet rule. I can't think of a way someone could have gotten in without a key. Mom, my beloved Suzi died this morning. I am heartbroken, and I feel responsible, for if not the landlord, then who? I have no enemies that I know of. How could I have been so arrogant to think I didn't have to obey the rules? I hope someday I can forgive myself. I will write again when I feel better. Don't worry about me.

Love, Michael

August 7
Dear Mom, I have done nothing but sleep and cry. I am too sick at heart to eat. Ironically, last week, on the very day Suzi died, it was reported that Stephen King warned J. K. Rowling not to kill Harry Potter in her final novel. In King's story, The Dead Zone, *he had a character kick a dog to death and received more letters of complaint than ever. His response?* "You want to be nice and say, 'I'm sorry you didn't like that,' but I'm thinking to myself number one, he was a dog not a person, and number two, the dog wasn't even real. I made that dog up. It was a fake dog, a fictional dog, but people get very, very involved." *Well, I say, Yes, Stephen King, they do. Dog is man's best friend. Suzi was not a fake dog, a fictional dog. She was a real dog, and she was mine.*

Love, Michael

August 14
Dear Mom, No, mother, don't worry...I won't seek revenge, although I must admit the idea did occur to me. I'm packing up my stuff and moving out of this godforsaken place. My next house will be pet friendly. I want Suzi back. If I want it badly enough, will it happen? Do you believe in reincarnation? Suzi changed my life—I will get another dog in her honor. I'll write stories that make our world a better place. Suzi

has been my inspiration. I may even dedicate my first novel to her.
Love, Michael

I've been running carefree through the clouds with my old friends since I got to puppy heaven. I've been told that, since I experienced such a dreadful death, and had already begun to change Michael's life, I will now be allowed to return to Earth as a human in order to make a difference in the world. The catch is this: I will not remember anything about past lives, nor will I know what my purpose is. I will have to figure it out as I grow. That's the way it is with humans. The choice is mine.

Michael is moving to another house, and he paid an extra month's rent as a pet deposit. He's looking online at a husky with a litter due any day now. In that litter will be a male with a rare, silver coat. When Michael sees it, he will want him. I need to make sure Michael stays on task, so I'm coming back as a silver male husky. I'm going to make the world much better through Michael, one person at a time. That's the way it's done on Earth.

"–not even a mouse."

by
Jeanine Baumgartle

Since I am no more than a quote from a popular myth, the term "even," admittedly, and at first glance, sets me apart even further from this story. Why mention me at all, unless there is a role to be filled, a connection to the imagination that nothing else could bridge? I think I am "alive," after all, in this context.

Every where and when and one is a context. As I drowse quietly in the woodwork, the sensitivity of my whiskers causes them to register minute changes in the displacement of air: Santa's activity in the next room, the drop of a stocking, the retrieval of the crumpled list from his pocket, to check his memory. There is a hearth; a father who makes sure of what is happening in his house at night; a family who sleeps in his care; a secret guest bearing gifts and good wishes for all the world. This scene is ornamented with dreams and candy and toys, all symbols of having more than enough. The animals–the reindeer bearing the sleigh–all have names, and immediately respond to what is asked of them. The moon illuminates the mystery and wonder.

Beyond those of us merely written down, is the historical, the actual events that prompt this cultural device, which attempts to elucidate the emergence of a new concept: love, hope, peace, for all. This portrait, too, has events that spiral into one epiphany, the need, the yearning of mankind revealed in the usual over-wrought brush strokes, sense splashed from chaos through true characters being who they are. Which is only Mary and her husband and baby, and astronomers, and sheep herders, and innkeepers. Animals are there, too, warm, waiting creatures, you see, just like me.

And you, in the plane of existence called the present, probably have some of my post-mythical descendants nearby. I wish no more for them than your awareness that they live and experience and die, just like you. Who knows what holds apart story and reality? Perhaps we will meet. But now, I must return to the woodwork, the tiny heartbeats and shallow breaths assigned to those of us whose only function is to be ready to wake.

Joy Kirchgessner *Sharp-Shinned Hawk* acrylic on canvas 16"x20"

He Tells Me I Cannot Love the Raven

by Marian Allen

It's ugly — ill-disposed — a scavenger —
haunter of graveyards, heartless, ghastly, grim,
unlovable, he says, it cannot love
me back, nor any other living thing.

He thinks I have some kindly bird in mind —
a trickster, spirit guide or Gothic prop —
He says I'm too upbeat to comprehend
the raven in his heart. This much is true.

I only know my own: Bitter and bleak,
oblivious to honor, grand design
or noble sacrifice, he doesn't soar
above the carnage life leaves in its wake.

He perches on a corpse and tears its flesh.
This eye is dark. *This* mother's son is meat.
"*This* one," he caws, "and *this* one, and, one day,
'this one' will be you, cold beneath my claws."

Violet, Mildred, Kenneth, Hazel, George,
Ruby — the list gets longer by the year
of those who've left me paralyzed with loss —
I see them in the glitter of his eye.

He feeds on mortality. In him, death is life.
Both are a moving banquet, a great feast
where death knell rhymes and chimes with dinner bell.
This is my raven, and I love him well.

Now You Sea God, Now You Don't
by
T. Lee Harris

The water was almost too hot. Josh Katzen sighed happily and slid down into the bath until the herb-scented suds from the body wash lapped at his chin and his long, sandy hair floated free around his shoulders. Since the tub was small, this made his knees poke out of the warm frothiness into the cool air of the bathroom. He groaned, tucked his legs around in a pseudo lotus position and settled in for a soak. He truly loved his work as an archaeological artist and photographer, but this was one pleasure he missed when he was on the dig in Peru. Sure, a couple times a season, he had a foray into Trujillo, and there was always the hotel in the nearby town of Piedras Rojas, but it wasn't home.

Closing his eyes, he pushed all thoughts of pencils, brushes, artifacts and dust from his head. He willed his body to relax, to – downstairs, a pot lid rattled. He opened one eye. The chicken had been simmering for better than thirty minutes, surely the pan would be way too hot....

The deep KLOOONNNG of a heavy Revere Ware lid hitting the kitchen floor launched him from the bath and toward the door with a bellow. Pausing to jam his arms into his ratty kimono, he pelted down the stairs. "Damn you! All of you! This I didn't miss in Peru!"

The kitchen was empty except for the pan lid rocking gently on the linoleum and a splotchy trail of broth that led to the living room, across the parquet to the couch. Which was growling.

Dropping to hands and knees he peered under and met a pair of unblinking, unrepentant green eyes. Boudicca. Of course. They had a stare-off until the little calico cat broke cover and tried to dart past him, clutching her prize of a still-steaming chicken wing in her teeth. He was ready for it and snagged her by the scruff of the neck, pinning her to the floor and snatching the piece of chicken. She sat up, irritably ruffling black-smudged apricot fur. Hearing lapping, he looked around and saw the two male cats, Whozits and Flash, had oozed out of their hidey holes. They were busily cleaning the broth their sister had so thoughtfully served up.

"Cats. Why do I even like you?" He shook the mauled chicken wing at them. "Well, this you forfeit, cat creeps."

As he stood to toss the wing in the trash, his gaze fell on the light table and the unfinished drawing surrounded by glossy photographs of the gleaming mask of the Moche sea god. The golden splendor drew him to it as surely as the fragrant chicken broth drew the cats.

Another cat face snarled out from the illustration board and the photos. A cat face of pure gold with inlaid teeth and startling blue eyes surrounded by eight tentacles of an octopus tipped with tongue-flicking snake heads. It was a riveting piece with a convoluted history. Made to adorn the brow of an ancient Moche king, it was looted from a northern Peruvian tomb in 1988. It then disappeared, only to be recovered by Scotland Yard from a dusty file cabinet in the offices of a prestigious London law firm almost twenty years later. Where had it been? No one knew or was saying. If the mask could talk ... ah, it probably wouldn't tell. It *was* part cat, after all.

The mask was making its way back to Peru, where it would take a place of honor in the Museo Nacional. It was making a brief stopover in Chicago, though, for noted Field Museum metal conservator, Dr. Morton Flores, to do an analysis of its condition and to make recommendations for its conservation. In the hour Josh had been permitted with it, it looked in excellent condition, but he was no metallurgist. He was an artist and a very lucky one to be allowed to photograph the piece. The drawing he was making from those photos would be a welcome addition to his growing portfolio.

He'd practically stood on his head to get permission, too. His association with Dr. Avi Rosenberg and the ongoing Piedras Rojas excavation carried a lot of weight, but Morty Flores didn't like him much. That was okay; he wasn't a member of the Flores fan club, either. There was just something there that sent his hackles up. He grinned. Maybe Morty felt the same way. It didn't matter. He'd gotten the okay from the museum board. He didn't sign Flores' paycheck any more than Morty signed his. Come to that, he didn't *have* much of a paycheck in the off seasons unless he sold his work.

He replaced the lid on the pot, secured it, then hurried upstairs to dress. At the rate the cats were going, there wouldn't be much to clean when he got back down. That was fine. What he really wanted was to get back to the drawing.

The drawing was progressing well. Josh alternated between staring at it from the kitchen door and dropping fresh-cut dumplings in boiling chicken broth.

He'd set the mask against a mud brick wall and offset it with a few pots from roughly the same time frame. It was working but ... maybe a little more dark to the right and the bottom? It needed more weight. The insistent chime of the doorbell pulled him reluctantly away wiping floury hands on a dishtowel.

There was a time when finding Colonel Vaughn DeVries of U.S. Military Intelligence standing on his doorstep would have elicited a different response. That was a long time ago. Today all he could muster was: "Oh shit."

"Hi, Katzen, good to see you, too." Seeing no move to let him in, he continued, "That mask you took pictures of Wednesday disappeared out of the museum workshop last night."

"I didn't do it."

"Man, that's a reflex."

Josh thudded his head against the doorframe. "Yeah. It is." He stood back to let DeVries in.

The entry led directly into the kitchen, which was comfortably warm after the crisp autumn afternoon. Josh headed to the stove where the pot steamed delicious smells into the air. He pulled a round loaf of bread from the oven, deposited it on a cooling rack and turned back to his visitor. "Okay. I am very upset that the mask has gone missing again. Permit me an Indiana Jones moment when I say that piece doesn't belong in a private collection; it belongs in a museum. I take it from the fact I'm not hearing ten types of screaming, that it's being hushed up for now?"

"Yeah, as you say, for now. The museum would like to get to the bottom of it quietly and the U.S. government hopes to oblige. When the higher ups saw that you'd been to the workshop and took pics of the thing, they thought you might be able to poke around and see if anything looks different."

"You mean other than the mask being gone?"

"Yeah, other than that." DeVries eyed him. "Listen, what are you so pissy about? You've done this before."

"That was someone else entirely. I'm not that person any more, Vaughn, remember? I'm simply Joshua Aaron Katzen, humble, yet lovable artist. Going in there as a special investigator would sort of ruin that, don't you think?"

"Aw, it's nothing like that! We worked too hard to build your new identity for that. We thought a private look, maybe?"

"Ooooooooh. You simply want me to break into the Field Museum for you? Well why didn't you say so? No."

"It's an unusual circumstance. We need your special talents."

"That's what you said the last time."

"And it worked fine the last time, didn't it?"

Josh glared and jabbed at the contents of the pot with a wooden spoon.

DeVries lifted hands in surrender. "Hey, don't bite my head off, Josh. It's an official request. I'm only the messenger. The Peruvians just got their shiny thingummy back. It would look pretty bad for Uncle Sam if that same shiny thingummy went missing on American soil now."

"And you are going to explain this to the museum officials if I get caught?"

DeVries snorted. "You only got caught once."

"And I've been paying for it twenty years, give or take."

There wasn't any way to respond to that. The Intelligence agent folded his arms and took the opportunity to look the place over. He and Katzen had worked together before, but that was in Peru. This was the first opportunity he'd had to view the animal in its den. Pretty nice den, too. The house itself was a simple floor plan, but Josh had put his unmistakable stamp on it so it more resembled a small museum than your average suburban Chicago residence. Then he saw the work on the board. "Wow. That's it, isn't it?"

Katzen came alive. DeVries was always amazed at the change when art or archaeology were involved.

Katzen said, "Yeah, that's it. It's an amazing thing, huh? These photographs and the drawing...? They fall short of the reality."

"Yep. Hey, I agree with you that this belongs to everybody, not just some collector with a big bankroll. Trouble is, if you don't help right now, right when it's happened, this fella might disappear for another twenty years or more."

Josh sighed. "I know."

"You'll do it?"

The artist's gaze swept the comfortable studio space, the cats in a furry heap on the couch, the bookcases lining the big room, and his frown deepened. "Why is it that the greater good always has the potential to ruin my life?"

DeVries looked like he was holding his breath until Katzen said, "Yeah, I'll do it."

"Awesome! It's gonna work great, you'll see. This will make the folks in DC *real* happy." He paused. "You gonna cut that bread?"

Katzen glided silently down the darkened stairway and stepped into the hall. It had been too easy to get in. He'd have to find a way to point out the vulnerability without seeming to. Granted, special skills were needed to do what he'd done, but he wasn't the only person around with those skills. He knew that all too well. People with his skills didn't usually mess with museums, though. The items in museum collections were too well known and once you got in, there were so many things that could go wrong – like the light being on in Flores' office and the door being open to the hall.

He stepped deeper into the shadows, fuming. Damn the man. The bastard had been making his life miserable from the git-go. His concern was understandable, but the way he'd fluttered and mother-henned the mask, it was a wonder that Josh had gotten a single decent photo of it. And the assistant! It was amazing, but Flores had managed to find an assistant even more annoying than himself. The kid, John Pennington, was a grad student who was learning hands-on conservation techniques at the museum. The day of the shoot, he was supposed to have been cleaning plaster casts of Egyptian statuary in the museum's collection. "Supposed" to were the operant words. What he'd actually done was bedevil Josh about his lighting set up, positioning of the mask and choice of cameras. It had been hard, but Katzen had finally managed to shut out the real world and hit the zone where he and the Moche sea god were alone. Then it flowed. Then it was right and he shot a full memory stick before the spell broke.

He smiled to himself. Notice if anything in the workshop was different? Like he'd noticed the workshop. Still, he'd lay money that the mask never left the museum. For something that large, it would be far easier to hide it right under everyone's noses until the hooha died down. Then, you just walk out with it when they're beating the bushes elsewhere. If he were going to hide something that size – Oops. Someone was coming up the stairs in back of him.

Glancing around quickly, he spotted a door that looked to be connected to a storeroom off the main workshop. It was unlocked, and he eeled into the dark room with its odors of plaster dust and cleaning solutions. Leaving the door open a crack, he angled for a clear view of the hall – right into something hard. He started, then recognized a partially cleaned plaster cast of Bastet with her sistrum clutched to her chest. Grinning up in the gloom, he breathed, "Cool. No better place for a cat to take refuge."

Just as hope was dawning that the footsteps would pass on to another floor, the stairwell door opened and John Pennington stepped out. Interesting. A grad student should have no business here this time of night. This was definitely worth watching. Or was it? Pennington turned and strode purposefully for Katzen's storeroom. Josh ducked farther behind Bastet and looked frantically for a place to hide, then his attention was drawn back to the hall by a coarse whisper, "There you are, you little shit cake. I figured I'd catch you skulking around tonight."

Josh didn't need to see the speaker to know who it was. It was Dr. Flores, but he wasn't addressing Josh. Penninton's reply sounded self-assured. "Hi, Doc. I wouldn't call it skulking. I was just coming in to finish work on that Egyptian cat goddess."

"Don't bullshit me. What did you do with it?"

"I don't know what you're talking about, Dr. Flores. I only came to finish cleaning that plaster cast of Bast. You said we needed it tomorrow. So they could set up the new show?"

"Bullshit. Don't bullshit me."

"Look, I don't...."

Katzen leaned forward. Yep. This was getting real interesting.

Flores interrupted. "You probably think you've scored big. Well, you're wrong. Look, you idiot, do you think they'd contact a student before trying the head of the department?"

Uncertainty crept into Pennington's voice, "Uhhhh. Who's 'they', Dr. Flores?"

Morty Flores never got the chance to answer as the elevator dinged and the door slid open. "Oh. Dr. Flores. Everything okay up here, sir?"

Great. One of the night watchmen. Katzen glanced up at Bastet, serene with her sistrum. *Getting crowded in here.*

Flores recovered well. "Yes, Hayworth, everything is fine. Pennington, here, came in to do some last minute work, but it turns out it wasn't needed. He was just heading out again."

Hayworth said, "Okay, want me to let you out the back way, John? Be closer than the side door you got the key for."

Pennington looked as stiff from Josh's vantage point as he sounded. "Yeah, that'd be great, Hay. Thanks."

The shadow that was Morty Flores stood motionless as the elevator door dinged and cut off Hayworth's casual banter. Then he barked an unpleasant laugh. "Clean the cat goddess. My ass." He closed the storeroom door firmly and stalked back to his office, muttering to himself.

Katzen released the breath he'd been holding and sagged against the goddess' unyielding leg. Close one. Some people got off on the adrenaline rush from encounters like that. He didn't. He listened as Flores paced and muttered in his office. Not good. If he wasn't leaving, it was only a matter of time before he came back this way. Most likely to do a search of his own. He obviously didn't know where the piece was and sounded convinced Pennington did. Well, the kid could have been there to finish cleaning the cast. Yeah. He could have ... nah. Josh grinned, patted his protectress and slid out into the hall. If he hustled, he could make it down to the side lot in time for Pennington to be escorted out.

In the parking lot, Pennington behaved oddly. He seemed his old self as he waved goodnight to the security guard and strode across the macadam. As soon as the door closed and he deemed himself alone, he scowled and veered off toward the street. He never went near a car. Instead, he wandered, at times aimlessly, at times feinting back toward the museum, then stopping abruptly and walking away again. Josh was considering the benefits of a nice solid brick when the man reached some sort of internal decision and headed off with a purpose. Josh struck out behind him, keeping to the shadows and cursing Vaughn DeVries soundly both for getting him into this and on general principles.

The graduate student's path took him straight to a crowded night spot, a multi-level bar popular with the college crowd. Katzen followed Pennington through several areas, stopped, bought a watered-down scotch and followed some more. Finally, they wound up in a central open air courtyard where the music from the various stages met in a mish mash of semi-identifiable sound and the surrounding shrubbery gave a false sense of privacy. All-in-all a good place for a meet. As his target moved farther into the hedge maze, he took the high road, mounting the stairs for the wooden catwalks that crisscrossed the gardens.

For a moment, Josh thought he'd lost his mark, but then he spotted him talking to two tall, dark men near the center fountain. Edging closer, he could tell the conversation was going badly for Pennington. The self-assurance was starting to slip and the two men were getting edgy. Not good. Suddenly Pennington stiffened and Katzen saw the glint of steel through the darkness. DeVries would kill him if he let the quarry go down like that. He didn't want to consider what the D.C. folks would say. Without a second thought, he moved directly over the tableaux, swung a leg onto the rail and dropped over the side.

The man with the knife oofed and flattened under Katzen's weight. Katzen came up with a fist under the other man's chin, using his momentum as he sprang to his feet for extra force. The man staggered backward and Josh brought his foot against the side of his head for good measure. Both were down, but they wouldn't be for long. He grabbed Pennington's jacket and pelted down the graveled path toward the street, dragging the student behind him.

Pennington never lost his deer-in-the-headlights look as he was towed across the street and down an alley until they came to a breathless stop. Katzen glanced over his shoulder. The student goggled, "Who? Josh?"

Katzen's head swug around. "Shut up and that's Mr. Katzen to you." He glanced over his shoulder again. They weren't following. Yet. Turning back, he demanded, "Where'd you leave your car?"

"But..."

"You didn't skateboard here tonight. Where did you *park*?"

"A block behind the museum."

"Fine." Katzen grabbed the jacket again and ran; throwing back, "Keep up. If you lag behind, I'll let them have you."

Pennington kept up.

At the car, Katzen held out his hand, demanding the keys. He watched Pennington weigh his options. Josh was smaller and older, but he had just taken out two guys Pennington's size without apparently breaking a sweat. In reality, his lungs were burning and his knees and back were sending him dire warnings of aches to come, but the kid didn't have to know that. He returned Pennington's unwavering stare. Reluctantly, the younger man fished the keys out of his jeans pocket and laid them in the artist's palm.

"Good choice," Josh said as he opened the driver's door. He nodded to the other side. "Get in."

Pennington was still cowed as they pulled out into traffic and headed away from the museum. Josh glanced into the rearview mirror until he was satisfied no particular headlights were a constant. Then he relaxed and said, "We have a while. Care to tell me why you nicked the mask of the sea god?"

The student started to bluster. Katzen snapped, "Cut the crap. You took it. I know you took it. Tell me why. NOW."

The bluster left and the other man collapsed into the car seat, scrubbing at his face with his palms and looking very young. Finally, he said, "Things haven't been going so good for me. I got messed up with someone I thought was a friend. She got me into drugs, broke up my marriage ... it's a soap opera. You don't want to hear it."

Katzen grunted noncommittally and swung the car onto the toll way.

Pennington sighed and continued. "Anyway, these guys showed up at school and they offered me a lot of money to steal the mask for them. Said I didn't need to know who or where, just that their employer had very deep pockets.

"Must be true, the wad they gave me as a retainer could choke a horse. At first I said no way, but then, I got to thinking about it and it was easy. I knew I could lift the thing and no one would be the wiser where it went. So I sort of did it and it went smoother than I even thought it would. Until I went back to pick it up and deliver it."

Katzen glanced at his passenger. They were headed toward Wisconsin and the kid was getting worried again. Good. "And...?"

"And I couldn't get to it tonight. I was real pissed off for a while, then I realized it might be a blessing in disguise."

"Mmmmm. Told the buyers you wanted more money, did you?"

"Guess I got a little greedy." They were in the suburbs and houses and streetlights were becoming fewer. "They got a little upset with me. Good thing you were at the tavern, huh?"

Without a word, Josh pulled into a darkened strip mall, drove around the back and parked in a far corner. He turned and treated Pennington to a long stare.

"Uhhhh. Josh ... Mr. Katzen? Why were you at the tavern?"

"I wondered when you'd get around to asking that. I followed you from the museum."

"No way! I was looking."

"Not good enough."

"Oh my god. You're a cop."

Katzen laughed. "Far from it. Let's just say there are people who take a dim view of such a high profile and valuable item going missing on their watch." He got out of the car, then as if by after thought, leaned back in, saying, "Oh, if they offer you a deal, I suggest you take it."

"Deal? Who?"

The passenger door opened and a broad man in a dark suit said, "Mr. Pennington, please step out and away from the car."

Josh leaned in the kitchen doorway swirling an ice cube in a couple ounces of Glenlivet and staring critically at the drawing. Yeah. It was finished. He worked kinked shoulders and sipped the amber liquor, savoring the burn as it went down.

The doorbell rang again. He wasn't surprised to see DeVries standing there this time and stood back to let him in. In the kitchen, he topped off his scotch and poured another for his visitor. Handing the glass over, he asked, "So do we get to live happily ever after now?"

"Some of us do. There's gonna be a lot of unhappily for Mr. Pennington in the near future."

Katzen nodded and sipped at his drink.

DeVries watched him and commented, "You really don't like the kid, do you?"

"I can't say that." He shrugged. "He's an arrogant bastard who thinks he's smarter than everyone else in the world. I find that annoying, but ... everyone deserves a second chance if they'll accept it."

DeVries started to say something, then frowned and sighed. Then he brightened a bit. "Aren't you going to ask where the thingummy was?"

"It was under Bastet."

"What? Why... How... Did that little jerk tell you? He said he hadn't."

Josh grinned. "No, it just made sense."

"I hate when you do that. It's always like watching a guy pull a rhino out of a baseball cap."

"It's what you guys used to pay me for."

DeVries nodded, straightened and looked around. "Hey, got any more of those dumplings? I'm starved."

Out of the Cradle

by

Marian Allen

I learned my lesson about the land when I was not much bigger than these youngsters. I had only hatched four months earlier and was barely swimming on my own, but I thought I knew as much as any of the grown merfolk.

"Stay away from the beach!" the old ones warned us, over and over, and we paid as little attention as these youngsters do now.

I hear myself echoing the cry I scoffed at when I was just a tad: "Stay away from the beach!" I dart between the mertads and the treacherous land, and slap my tail on the water's surface.

I ought to let them take their chances, but I'm always more protective if I've happened to be there when the tads hatch, as I was with these. I worry more, and do more than my share of the minding. The stress makes me feel older than my seven years. Every day, I find more white hairs on my head and more silver scales on my tail. Sometimes I wonder if it's worth the trouble—but I know it is. When I see mertads playing, leaping free of the ocean, grasping at one another's hands or fins, their hair streaming behind them, I could weep for joy.

...And I order them back to the deeps.

The day I was telling about, the day I learned how little I knew, I had just turned four months, so I would have been about the size of an old one's palm.

It was a day when the upper sky sprayed its weird, flavorless water into the rich broth of the lower sky, the sea. Waves were high. Everyone over three months old played in the whitecaps, letting the swells lift them and then sliding into the wave troughs. Parents patrolled the deeps, guarding against predators—sharks and rays who love nothing more than a quick snack of merfolk too young to give them trouble.

I had been warned many times to stay clear of the strand, but I was sure my elders were just timid or dull or stupid, or were mindlessly repeating meaningless nonsense just because they had been told it when they were young. I could see the water roll onto the shore, then drag out to sea. It looked like it would be tremendous fun to ride a wave in and back—and absolutely safe.

I rode in, but my expected easy landing was a savage *thump!* The air was forced from every bladder in my body and I was left gasping on the damp sand. Panicked, I thrashed and flopped, and felt myself fall blissfully into salt water.

But I was not in the ocean. I was in a tide pool, cut off from safety by a wall of rock. Worse, I was not alone. With me was one of our young's deadliest enemies—a crab. It was over twice my size as I was then, and I was completely at its mercy.

I cried for help but I was too far from the deeps for anyone to hear my tiny airborne voice, and no one could have come to me if they had heard.

The crab darted at me. I dodged, scooping sand from the bed of the tide pool with my tail and flicking it into its eyes. That slowed it down for a few seconds, but there was nowhere for me to swim, nowhere to hide, no way to escape. All I could do was evade, with capture and death at the end. It lunged at me again, pincers snapping. I twisted away, but it caught me by the hair. I strained against its grip, but it was bigger and stronger than I was. With sickening ease, it drew me toward its mandibles, ready to rend me with its other claw and stuff the pieces into its foul belly.

An ear-splitting noise from above nearly drove the crab from my mind. A gigantic creature towered at the rim of the tide pool, blocking the sun. It had two extra arms where its tail should be. Its neck, where it should have had gills, was hideously smooth. It was the real-life monster the old ones use to frighten naughty tads—the Drylander!

It made another noise and scooped up the crab, with me still dangling by the hair from one pincer.

I had never seen a Drylander so close before, though the old ones always claimed the monsters could swim, and every old one knew somebody who knew somebody who had either drowned one or saved one's life.

This one turned the crab to get a better look at me, and my captive captor took the opportunity to nip the hand that held it.

With a roar, the Drylander flung the crab—with me still attached— out to sea. The two of us swam through the air over the heads of my spawnmates who had gathered thick as algae. As if in a dream, I watched the Drylander suck its wounded hand and dance on its lower arms.

We plunged into the ocean, and the deeps had never felt so good! I had hoped the crab would lose its grip on me when we hit, but my hair was tangled around its claw.

I cried out again. Now that I was undersea, the vibrations of my wail pierced the water and brought my mother and father. They were both young but full-grown, as much bigger than the crab as the crab was bigger than I.

So, instead of him making a meal of me, dinner went the other way around. My parents are very fond of crab, which saved me from punishment for my foolhardy disobedience.

That was the day I learned to believe the old ones' warnings—to stay out of the shallows and away from the land. But does it do me any good to tell my young ones that? I might as well be talking to the reef.

Joy Kirchgessner *White-Tailed Deer: Safe Passageway*
acrylic on canvas 18"x24"

Deer

by
Jeannine Baumgartle

The tawny head lifts,
stares toward the building.
Did you see something, Mama?
Yes, I did, my little twins.
Come over here, in the grass
next to me. If you look
up the hill, to that building,
the second window
in the second story-
yes, there it is again-
a face; see it? It appears
from time to time; you
just have to be watching.
What does it do there, Mama?
Oh, what everything does,
I suppose, eat and sleep.
Is there grass in there?

Without water or sun—
I doubt it. They bring in
lots of white rustley lumps,
perhaps that is their food.
I think they must be
rather delicate creatures.
They do not walk
often, or very far,
and they have to be
carried in the mouths
of those glass-eyed fake
lives, with shells like bugs.
-We will not get close to those.
Do they play, Mama?
Yes, I think they do,
as fawns. Still, I think
I would not play with them.
They play with dogs.

Contributors

The Southern Indiana Writers Group has been more-or-less together since 1992. We began meeting monthly in a conference room in a local hospital. We now meet weekly to exchange information and expertise on everything from computers to poetry. The group also serves as a critique forum (in the same sense that a pack of wolves serves as food critics). Membership is limited, but visitors are welcome, and have been known to fit in so well they become members against their better judgment.

Bonnie Abraham After twenty-five plus years of writing letters disqualifying people from Unemployment Benefits, she retired in order to write something more pleasant. She writes short stories (many with Biblical themes), poetry and devotionals. Currently, she resides in Corydon with her mother's ghost.

Marian Allen lives in a big house in a little wood, which is not the only difference between Allen and Laura Ingels Wilder. Allen has three novels on electronic disk (alternatively known as "coasters"). She has published stories in print and on-line magazines, including Marion Zimmer Bradley's FANTASY Magazine, The Phone Book, PanGaia and Oceans of the Mind.

Jeannine Baumgartle writes poetry and fiction. Her work has appeared in publications such as *Green Meadow Press*, *Flying Island, Literally*, and Studio: *A Journal for Christians Writing* and won a residency for poetry at the Mary Anderson Center for the Arts . She and her husband live in the small town of Crandall.

Ginny Fleming doesn't know the meaning of the word "Fear." The pages "F" through "G" are missing from her Funk & Wagnal. Credits include three optioned sitcom scripts, two movie scripts traveling on a slow train around Hollywood and a novel under consideration. She traces her roots to Milltown (Miller-Perkins) and leaves her heart in Sarasota.

Joanna Foreman has one main claim to fame: She has successfully raised three sons and has two grandchildren who are still too young to be anything less than perfect. She writes both short fiction and slice-of-life vignettes, and is currently putting the finishing touches on her first novel. Until recently, she had been too timid to submit her writing for publication. Now, she eagerly watches her mailbox for rejection slips. She and her husband, Craig, married barefooted on St. Augustine Beach in 2001. They built a modest home in the middle of two wooded acres in Georgetown, Indiana, where they will live happily ever after.

Dirk Griffin has written theatre reviews for *Arts Kentuckiana*, had a script produced for Public Access Television, and has written music/lyrics and/or scripts for several musicals. Bunbury Theatre of Louisville, Kentucky, selected one of his plays to include in their 2001 15th Anniversary 15 Minute Play Festival.

T Lee Harris is a writer and illustrator who has been a lover of mystery and the detective genre since discovering books. A graduate of Indiana University with a Bachelor of Fine Arts, T has been involved with radio production, game design, comic books and desktop publishing. Interests include participation in the Society for Creative Anachronism and Renaissance Faires, tailoring authentic costuming for re-enactors and playing online roleplaying games. Several novels are in progress featuring Sitehuti and Nefer-Djenou-Bastet, Josh Katzen and a series set in ninth century Ireland.

Jane E. Jones truly has her head in the clouds. (She lives so high on a hill she can see the Tunder-Over_louisville fireworks from 40 miles away.) She shares her aerie with one husband, three dogs, seven horses, and a herd of cats. She's been a legal secretary for twenty-plus years and uses writiing to escape from the long-winded legalese she deals with daily. She writes romantic adventures and paranormal fiction and is currently working on the final installment of a three-novel series.

Joy Kirchgessner is a business woman, illustrator and writer. Her Paintings were recently on tour with the Kentucky National Art and Wildlife Exhibition. She shares her home with her husband and two horses.

Glenda Mills resides with her husband, three children, and the mortal remains of four dogs, a cat, various hamsters, turtles, frogs and fish in Floyd County, IN. When she is not busy being a "stay-at-home" mom, which is seldom, she enjoys writing poetry, non-fiction and fiction. Her work crosses genres and presently includes short stories, poems, a finished manuscript on an introspective look at the miscarriage of her child, and an unfinished manuscript of a "slightly" psychotic female serial killer. She firmly belives that variety is the spice of life.

Carole Wyatt lives with her husband and children sandwiched between soybean fields and a cemetery. She measures the seasons by crop growth and grave decorations. When she isn't working in the organic market and dairy, she writes. She recently took second place in the Aspiring Writers Contest with her short story, "The Letter." Her novel, *Weather Swans*, took third place in the 2006 Platinum Fiction Contest. The newest stories in print are "On Rodent Feet" in *Cup of Comfort for Weddings* anthology and "Special Delivery" in the *Blink* anthology. Her true-life anecdotes have appeared in *Brave Hearts, Rocking Chair Reader and Small Town Journal.* Carole also works as a book reviewer for Novelspot.com.

Previous Publications by Southern Indiana Writers

Indian Creek Anthology
Ghost Writers
Christmas Bizarre
Dragon: Our Tales
Grounds for Suspicion
2000 Tales
Way Out West
Unbridled Lust
There's Something Under the Bedtime Stories
Novel Ingredients
Write of Passage
Off the Rack

Coming in 2007

IT'S ALWAYS SOMETHING

Ever have one of those days?

Visit our web site for excerpts of previous publications
and availability information:

http://siw.artisanpath.com